THE SILENT MONOLITH

A NOVEL BY

ELIOT TAYLOR

The Silent Monolith

Copyright © 2024 by Eliot Taylor

ISBN: 979-8-3306-5812-1 (Paperback)

Cover Design: Eliot Taylor, Edited with *Canva*

Editing: Eliot Taylor

Illustrations: Eliot Taylor

Printed & distributed by: IngramSpark

For permissions requests, please contact:

- Eliot Taylor
- eliottaylorllc@gmail.com

Dedication

To Yeshua, who is Yahweh, and His kingdom purpose through the impact of forgiveness, endurance of faith, and sacrificial love.

To my family and my bestie who stood by me through thick and thin.

To the Instagram writing community, through which I've met many talented poets and writers, and have read plenty of beautiful pieces.

Here's to a new story, a new chapter...

"The human heart has many faces.
Each facet is a glimpse into the countenance of the soul.
Yes, the human heart has many open doors and a plethora of windows.
So, who are you letting in?"

PROLOGUE

"Are you sure this is what you want?"

Those words echoed in her mind for six months.

No matter how much she tweaked, rearranged, or bargained, the question of motivations remained unavoidable. Each fleeting second was engulfed by a relentless tide of uncertainties, and each sleepless night was a descent into turmoil. Half a year later, the running met a dead end. She finally caved and slumped on her futon, which was a deep reddish-brown.

Was she truly fit to be a wife?

This was a question that no woman could truly answer.

Wifehood comes with many imaginations, as expectations often stir up impracticalities and legalism. Every era has seen its adaptation, but no clause or reformation has yet to confidently ease the qualms of marriage. Still, for some minds, especially ones like Ryland's, forevermore sounded like pleasure.

Just like that, all that she loved about Charlie and those nights of figuring each other out—even momentary tug-a-wars and estranged mornings—sparked an untamable fire. Her soft brown eyes were suddenly molten and laced with defiance. Her back straightened as she dug her heels in with feet firmly planted on the carpet floor.

Mama sat on the opposite end of the coffee table, bracing herself for impact. Her elongated, slender forelimbs draped over the arms of the deep, wine-padded chair as her midnight eyes commanded authority. But beneath all those layers of wisdom was a forty-year-old scorned heart, ready to give warmth wherever it was needed. Ryland would never know that.

"I'm not you," her scarlet-haired daughter refuted. Even Ryland was surprised at how steady her voice remained, as her words were even keeled. Uncertainty never left the 25-year-old, but the edge of grace was like breaking out of a chrysalis with new wings.

"I know an awful lot about marriage, honey," said Mama. She appeared unmoved by Ryland's sudden burst of confidence. To her, it was merely a sprint of luck against a long road of odds.

Ryland remained planted in her love for Charlie. She held onto it, shielding herself from her own doubts and the ghosts of her mother's past. "I understand that this is too touchy for you—" she let out, "—and I'm sorry that Dad made marriage a living hell. But we're talking about twenty-five years later, with a daughter who clearly has a head on her shoulders. This daughter fell in love with a man who believes just as much as she does. He wants what I want."

Mama didn't hold back her skepticism. She let out a derisive scoff with brows nearly raised to her hairline. "Unbelievable," she muttered under her breath. But her next words were undeniably aimed at Ryland. "And *you* want marriage?" she questioned. It was more condescending, like she knew the answer.

But it was the wrong answer. "If you truly knew me, you wouldn't have asked that."

"You don't even know what a good marriage looks like!" Mama protested. Finally, the steadfastness had dwindled, and her anxieties were louder than Ryland's. "Look around you!" she pressed. Her arms were raised in the air as she waved them about. "The apartment you love so much is now a storage unit! How can you even tolerate the stench of cardboard and packing tape so condensed in the air like this? Not to mention, you finally have your marriage counseling license now. I was betting on a new career opportunity for you—not changing your life for a guy!"

"I'm not changing my life for a guy!" argued Ryland. "I think we're at a decent pace for a *six-year relationship.* It's not like we're getting married tomorrow anyway!"

Mama turned her head away with a flying hand to the face, cupping her mouth. Her eyes glossed by the second as her gaze shifted to the window, staring at nothing. Her long, dark lashes captured a bronze accent in the sunlight. A tear finally gave way and tumbled down her freckled cheek as an avalanche of emotions finally burst through the façade.

But that was clockwork, and Ryland knew it.

The crimson-haired darling rose to her feet, having had enough of the voices screaming in her head. It was time to put them to rest. Maybe not all at once, but the brutal conversation was a start. "It's *you* who will never know anything about marriage," she said.

Deep inside, she was a scared little girl, afraid to take the leap. But she had to, for her sake. If bones were crushed after the fall, and if she too met the same demise, then who could she truly blame but herself?

Ryland watched Mama pull herself up. She glided to her daughter ever so carefully, afraid that the slightest misstep would send her running in the opposite direction. Ryland felt those familiar maternal hands finally clutch her shoulders. She met those pressing dark eyes and maintained her glare. "I'm getting married, and that's that," she said. But were those words meant for her mother?

Or for herself?

"Ryland?" a voice called out. Then a new set of hands gripped her shoulders and rocked them hard. Then harder...

And harder...

"Ryland... Ryland!"

Another stern shake and, "RYLAND!"

CHAPTER ONE

Ryland bolted upright, blindly lurching forward. Her forehead slammed against the dashboard as her bones felt like they might succumb to the unforgiving hardness of its unyielding force. The impact echoed such a skin-crawling thud that it triggered panic in Charlie. Cussing escaped Ryland's lips in fits of harsh breaths, but she was unaware of her own reaction. Disoriented by the pounding of her heart in her ears, she guided her neck cautiously as her head lifted slowly. Her eyes scanned all around her, allowing her senses to recalibrate. Then white-hot pain seared her temples like fire. She crumbled forward, but this time, her head collapsed in her hands. She let out a moan as frustration etched across her features. Finally, she noticed the rumbling beneath her—but a second too late. The rubber of tires against the dirt-packed pavement echoed a piercing shrill that bled into the stillness of the picturesque silence.

For a moment, the only sound was the delicate dance of uncertainty breathing in and out of her lungs.

A hand pressed the circle of her back as another wrapped around her.

"Ryland?" a familiar voice called to her again with such depth that even its husk was gentle on her. "Come on...

Talk to me...

Please?"

Lifting her head up once more, she had finally begun to piece together her surroundings. The cocoon of her dreamscape gradually blended into the reality of the desert landscapes. There was nothing but vast blue skies, heavy moisture in the air, and a scarcity of wildlife. The only other shield around them was the tin barrier of a dark gray Silverado. Solace seeped in as her eyes looked for Charlie's. His glistening, dark eyes were like open arms.

"I'm just out of it," Ryland told Charlie. "I think we've been out here for too long." She forced a smile, hoping it was enough to tame his mind.

He stared back at her, silently tracing her face for whatever he was looking for. Ryland almost fell into worry all over again, with every second dragging out his careful examination. Then, just like that, her nerves quieted when Charlie's features softened into a toothy smile. "You're an Arizonan, and the heat is getting to you?" he joked.

Ryland wanted to fire back with something witty, but all she could muster was a light laugh as the mixture of sweat and embarrassment painted her cheeks a deep rosy hue. Yet, she never missed the fleeting glimpse of doubt in his eyes. Neither of the two spoke about it. Instead, Charlie's arms dropped from around her as he pulled away to climb out of the car.

She watched him walk to the back doors with care etched all over his face. From the open door, he stretched a lean arm across the seats, reaching for the duffle bag they packed together that same morning. Ryland recounted all its continents, like trail mix, four accessible water bottles, a deck of solitaire cards, all the money needed for their trip, and, of course, the first aid kit on Charlie's mind. He plucked out a few tablets from a pack of Motrin and snagged one of the bottles and a granola bar.

Then he was back at her side in a flash.

Ryland was grateful to have something to relieve the tension that pounded the walls of her skull. She thanked him, then gobbled down the pills and granola. After several indulgent swigs of water, she relaxed back in the passenger seat, feeling more attuned to her pre-honeymoon adventure. She felt the weight of Charlie's gaze on her. She knew the look of peace on her face made her fiancé proud of himself.

She seized that moment to drink him in. She watched the gentle breeze play with his long, ebony locks, coaxing a few rebellious strands to frame his face. Her fingers traced the twin moles delicately positioned beneath his left eye, like the one last perfect touch. It was as though God had taken care to accentuate every contour and bone structure. Yet Charlie's beauty was just one facet. It was a mere plus to what captivated her. The warmth and compassion that radiated from within were qualities that eclipsed any external beauty.

A subtle quirk touched the corners of his lips as curiosity washed over his gaze. "What?" he inquired, his voice relaxed and soft.

Ryland dismissed it with a shrug, but the look on her face spilled it all. "Ready to hit the road again?" she countered with a smile.

Charlie slid back inside and shut the door after him. His hand grasped the key and pulled, coaxing the engine to life. Faint ticking sounds reverberated in the air, and the dashboard lights illuminated after a few blinks. With one hand on the gearstick and the other firmly on the steering wheel, he uttered, "I'm ready when you are."

Then, Charlie maneuvered the car back onto the road, with the intention of resuming their planned voyage through the desert.

The couple had finally abandoned their lives in Flagstaff, their hometown, about six hours ago. The sun had already perched itself high and shone its rays as they set off on the road. Ryland, now awake and upright, gazed about as Charlie's eyes fixed ahead. As the rubber of tires kicked up sun-drenched dust, which was a golden-red hue, Charlie started to gear the car toward his focus. He and Ryland would need a place to rest. Last time they checked the clock, it was nine in the morning, but this was back when they started to leave Flagstaff. At some point, they ended up in Holbrook, mostly for Charlie to visit Route 66. He prided himself on being a historic nerd and went as far as majoring in it to achieve his long-term dream ʇof archeology. Ryland observed him from the sidelines and as she leaned against the hood of his

Silverado. It was like watching a kid in a candy store for the first time.

She marveled at his connection to history and how each rusted relic seemed to unlock a different dimension of an era. Charlie's joy was a symphony of appreciation, unveiling through the curtains of the past. Even Ryland admitted to herself the testaments etched into every curve and site. But Charlie was her best point of view, as he stood like a silhouette in the amber glow. It was a rare moment of Americana, something that is hard to find in a generation deeply embedded in the digital space and has long lost its touch with the art of rarities. In that moment, it seemed their differences softened, and in the fading light, she remembered her love for him, which illuminated in his eyes as he gazed back at her. He was immersed in the scenery, for sure, but a second did not go by without her on his mind. He looked back to confirm that she was still around. Ryland gave him a nod of assurance as the air crackled with an unspoken understanding, a bridge between two souls navigating the vast complexities between them.

Time did not escape the two, especially Charlie, as Ryland started to show signs of weariness again. She only got like that when her sugar levels dropped. The thought of kissing the sighting goodbye did not dare knock on his mind, which Ryland was grateful for. Even more so when she let Charlie help her climb back inside his car.

Long after their tires hit the asphalt once more, civilization finally emerged into view. Twilight had already fallen when Charlie and Ryland reached the heart of Holbrook. The landscape shifted with such ease that Ryland was caught off guard by neon signs flickering in their separate directions toward their attractions. Although the area was not congested with people, Ryland did spot a few cars parked near the owner's motel spot for the night as some people fluttered through the doors of restaurants or shops. At some point along the journey, she rolled down the window for fresh air. As the breeze fingered through her loose ginger ringlets, it carried a savory aroma that kept her glued to the meal options passing by, causing her stomach to grumble.

Charlie stole a glance over his shoulder and shot a teasing look her way. He mumbled something that sounded close to a promise to get them food once he found a permanent rest stop. That drew Ryland's attention to a few spots they could try. She pointed a finger at one that sort of resembled a villa. "That looks promising," she remarked. Her stomach grumbled again, which made her cast pleading eyes at Charlie, like a child bargaining for their favorite treats. Thankfully, Charlie agreed with Ryland's pick and pulled into the parking spot. Soon after, he disappeared through the glass doors, where it was easy for Ryland to watch him interact with the clerk.

As she waited, a thought crossed her mind to check her phone. She and her mother still weren't on the best terms when she left Flagstaff. Her screen flickered on, sparking hope to find a message or two, but she was left disappointed. There were only a few notifications from her email and other apps she had on her phone. Ryland let out a shaky breath as the past months flooded her mind, like the pain of her mom not attending her wedding. That stung more than anything.

Ryland was so engulfed by these thoughts that she didn't notice the flying car door opposite her. Neither did she feel Charlie crawl beside her. It wasn't until his arms wrapped around Ryland that she was finally pulled back into the moment. "Hey..." Charlie called out so tenderly. His voice was so carefully laced with egis and devotion, ready to lick all her wounds and lift her up.

All she could muster was a half-hearted grin. But she didn't say much. Thankfully, for Ryland, Charlie made no attempt to press for anything. Instead, he muttered a joke about getting them some food before they resorted to the leather seats. That did conjure a laugh out of Ryland, but it was surely weakened. That's when she felt Charlie's fingers enlace with hers as they drove off to their next destination.

The drive around the area took about twenty minutes before the couple finally settled for a diner. Mostly because it was getting late, as the other reason was Ryland growing tired of the grumbling noises erupting from her stomach. She just wanted anything at that point. So, as they walked through the door, which jingled to announce their presence as new customers, she practically skipped to their chosen window booth and flung open the menus. Like clockwork, she found her favorite meal when she ate at any diner: a black bean burger, extra pickles, no tomatoes, and a side of fries. This diner advertised a special sauce they created to go with that order, and she was willing to try.

As the waitress marked down their orders, Ryland peeked over at Charlie, who couldn't keep his eyes off her. It was hard to tell if he was in his puppy-love mood again or utterly surprised that she added a slice of cheesecake and a large coke to her order.

In a split moment, Ryland's attention immediately redirected to the interaction between her fiancé and the waitress. It's not that she was the jealous type. Honestly, her mind was always preoccupied and too sagacious to play that game. She and Charlie had long ago developed trust. But not enough to keep nature at bay. It crept in occasionally to test the foundation built between the young couple, and tonight was just that opportunity. Ryland noticed a sudden gleam in the original boredom of the waitress's blue eyes. The redhead watched the careful twirl of those golden locks around her manicured finger and how her laugh pitched at something Charlie said, despite no clear cue of a joke. Ryland leaned back in her chair and aimed her stare at him. Yet Charlie was busy being attentive to his stomach to notice either woman in front of him.

Ryland let out an internal cheer when he finished, prompting the waitress to finally leave their table. She licked the tip of her upper teeth—something she often did when she was torn between ripping Charlie a new one and keeping the peace. She settled on the latter, considering that this trip was something of a pre-honeymoon for them, and it would quickly turn into hell if something like this dampened the mood. Ryland couldn't help the gleam of triumph within her when Charlie's gaze finally glued back on her, just the way she preferred. It was then that she decided to write off that moment of jealousy because of exhaustion. Yes, she needed food to boost her mood, but the honest-to-God answer for the insatiability was the feeling of Charlie's arms around her and the sound of his heart beating only for her. It does sound a bit selfish, but she sure as hell wasn't the type to share.

Just as his hand reached across the table and cupped hers, the same temptation found its way back to Ryland. Instead of the waitress, however, it was some other girl with messy dark hair that hung down her back. She wore what looked like shorts and an oversized band T-shirt. She flashed a glossy-lipped grin at the couple as her girlish voice carried throughout the diner with her chirped, "Hi!". Ryland registered the newcomer as just quirky and younger than her and Charlie, who were also barely past twenty-five. "I just wanted to say you two are so cute together!" she beamed childishly.

Once again, Ryland backed down. This was only because she caught some other vibes from the girl. It was something unsettling, but she couldn't put her finger on it. She peeked at Charlie, who appeared none the wiser but replied a polite "Thank you" with a healthy dosage of distance in his voice. Knowing how anxious he was around strangers, she could tell he really wanted to go back to just the two of them. So, it was up to Ryland to steer her away with carefully sugarcoated responses as the girl continued to chat with them.

The interaction lasted a few minutes. The girl pried about their origins and how she could tell they weren't from the area. She went on to name-drop hotspots to visit, which seemed to lengthen the conversation until she was finally interrupted by the waitress's arrival with the couple's order. "Oh, whoops! I've run my mouth again!" the girl bantered. "I'll let you two eat up! It was nice talking to you!"

Ryland and Charlie exchanged a look but were more grateful for a break. The waitress set their plates on their table and flashed one more smile at Charlie before heading off to help another table. Ryland almost commented on the whole debacle, but her stomach demanded attention. When she opened her mouth, it was only to dig into her meal.

CHAPTER TWO

"What was that all about back there?"

As Ryland stood before the fogged mirror, the residue of her lengthy shower cloaked the glass with a hazy reflection of her tired form. With one hand clutching a handful of wet tresses and the other pat-drying droplets that still clung to her shoulders, she caught enough of herself to see the branches of confusion etched across her features. Pausing mid-motion, she hesitated before stepping into the threshold that bridged their shared spaces, which was part bedroom, part dining area.

In the dimly lit room, she found Charlie seated on the floor with his phone screen in one hand and still clad in the clothes he wore earlier. Their eyes met in a familiar dance, a silent connection that creamed any attempt at words. A fluttering surge washed over Ryland as she gazed at him like the flicker of the butterflies fleeting in her stomach. Beneath the surface, a current of tension lingered as his words anchored in her mind.

Charlie's gaze held a knowing glint, though Ryland was still puzzled. "Back at the diner," he finally clarified.

The memory of their waitress's itching attempts at Charlie seeped into Ryland's mind, stirring resentment within her. Despite this, she tried to deflect with something close to a lighthearted jest. "A lot happened," she quipped.

Charlie's expression grew sullen. "No, that girl," he persisted. "There was something off about her..."

Guilt gnawed at Ryland's conscience as she recalled their interaction. The unease of their exchange resurfaced as regret slowly dripped into her. "Oh..." she murmured, drifting deeper in thought.

"You noticed the marks on her too, right?" Charlie added.

That alone jolted her conscience. "What?" she blurted. "Where did you see that?"

Gesturing toward his face and neck, Charlie pointed out the faded marks he noticed. "She had bruises on her neck and a scar on her cheek," he explained. "And her clothes... they looked jagged... I don't feel right going to sleep if..."

Lines spread across Charlie's face and became more apparent as he disappeared into his own mind. Something about this was a trigger, and Ryland knew exactly why. She flew to his side and made sure they were eye-to-eye. "If we see her again, we will help her," she vowed.

Charlie managed a slight nod but remained silent. He was too entangled in himself to articulate. Her hand lifted to his face as her fingers traced every inch of his tan skin. The fluttering feeling returned when he leaned into her embrace and rested his head on her shoulders. With every breath kissing her skin and each comb of her fingers sneaking into Charlie's soft, long strands, the passing moments of longing levied a potency between them. They stayed that way, resting in each other's arms. But the realization of her wet hair and tiredness seeping into Ryland and Charlie tugged their arms, forcing the couple to pull away. With a gentle touch and a lingering glance, they parted ways, each retreating into their respective spaces for the night, as an unspoken promise lingered in the air like a whispered prayer.

The following morning came with a cast of the sun's golden glow over the desert landscape. The couple had slept in a bit, still exhausted from a long night of wired emotions firing within themselves. Even so, Ryland and Charlie managed to step out of their motel room, ready to face the day ahead. As Charlie double checked the lock, Ryland's gaze floated to something hanging from their door. She let her hand trace a red string taped to the surface. A thought crossed her mind, but she shooed it away with a simple explanation. Maybe it was a part of a system behind the scenes of the hotel they stayed in. Before she could mention it to Charlie, he had already walked away, prompting Ryland to follow suit.

They settled for the same diner as the night before, considering that neither were in much of an exploration mood on an empty stomach. Unlike last night, they were greeted by a much older woman, who was strikingly resembling the classic American grandma, with her silver hair brushed back into a bun and rosy cheeks that made anyone's heart warm. Her voice carried out in a sing-song manner, which made both Charlie and Ryland grateful. But once their waitress was off to gather more orders, the atmosphere of hardened emotions slithered between them again. Ryland noticed the coldness more than ever, but it was Charlie who reached out. He lifted her hand and pressed his warm lips against her skin. He held it there for a moment, causing Ryland's heart to flutter like ever. Just like that, the ice receded into a budding warmth in her belly.

"Do you remember our third date?" Charlie asked.

Bemused, Ryland nodded as those memories sparked something in her. Back then, they were still sophomores in college, struggling between papers, exams, and just having a simple meal in their stomachs. Both were on work study and met during a conservatory event organized by the campus's student committee. It wasn't until early senior year that Charlie finally asked her out.

The first two dates were simplistic, allowing Charlie and Ryland to get their feet wet. The third date was their most memorable one, although it was not their only unforgettable experience. It was because they had finally explored a different side of their favorite commonality: nature. It was spontaneous too. That day, the skies poured into the earth, as it happened to be the same day as midterms. The storm only lasted until after they finished their exams.

Ryland and Charlie got out just in time to see the clouds roll back, allowing the sun to burst through the seams. Charlie came up with the random idea to follow the rainbow they saw forming in the sky. And so, they did. All along the forty-five-mile ride, they joked about finding gold until the pair finally approached the end of the rainbow. It led them to the outskirts of Flagstaff, where they uncovered a shimmering lake under the late afternoon sun. It was such a pristine blue that Ryland couldn't keep her eyes off it, completely unaware of Charlie's eyes on her. From that moment, she captured a new meaning for rainbows.

"That's something I'll never forget..." She said half to herself.

Abruptly, the aroma of butter, oil and sugar blended in the air begrudgingly yanked her back to the present moment. Thankfully, she had enough sat right before her to keep the sprinkles of such a fond memory as clear as day.

Charlie's eyes lit up. "Great! Then, I hope you're still into rainbows..."

"Why?" Ryland inquired with a slight furrow of her brows.

"Have you seen petrified wood before?"

Ryland shot him a baffled look, "What are you up to?"

Charlie began to ramble about a ranch he discovered online that was in the area. It was the kind where they could explore petrified wood. Before he went to sleep last night, he bought entry passes.

After breakfast, that was their destination of the day. The closer they got; the nervier Ryland became. Upon their arrival, they were greeted with a warm welcome from the hosts. Their shtick was being a family-owned business, equipped with a vast knowledge of wood, fossilization and botany. Ryland and Charlie walked up and down the pathways where they encountered plenty of stories behind each kaleidoscope of colors and textures. Each one earned its own marvel as its patterns and history were unearthed. The whole thing was so infectious. The splendor of it all felt unreal to Ryland.

Toward the end of their visit, Charlie and Ryland retreated to the entrance they came from, but not before Charlie got her a pretty moonstone ring from the gift shop. She filed this new memory to the back of her mind, as she always cherished the adventurous side of their relationship. She dearly hoped it was something they never forgot to do as the years passed on.

Back on the road, the couple shuffled around thoughts of heading back to their room or getting food first. They were still full of excitement, so they didn't have much of an appetite. If anything, Ryland simply wanted to enjoy the car ride with Charlie. On the other hand, they were thirty miles away from their hotel stay. As the sun slowly dipped in the horizon, finally depleting the bridge between the late afternoon and early evening with a blanket of peach, turquoise, and dark blue hues across the skies, Ryland's senses grew more sensitive to the road around them. She reminded herself of the shield that was Charlie's Silverado, which seemed to have eventually subsided her nerves. But her fiancé had already noticed.

"What's wrong?" he posed. His tone was soft but the quickness of it returned the alarming feeling in Ryland, who answered, "Nothing... just a little creepy being on the road this late."

Though she tried to joke, it didn't stop Charlie's baffled expression from indenting his features. "We were alone yesterday..." he mentioned.

Ryland shrugged it off. "Yeah, well..." she started. "I don't know. Ever since I saw that red string on our door—"

"What red string?" Charlie cut in. His usual even-keeled demeanor rapidly vanished as soon as Ryland mentioned the string. So much so that it left Ryland with a dilemma: should she talk about it?

Before Ryland executed her final decision, her eyes shifted to her right. Almost instantly, she spotted a terrifying glimpse in the side view mirror. She attempted to smother the yelp from escaping her lips. But it was too late.

"What?" Charlie pressed. "What's going on?" As he said this, his eyes flickered about until they finally rested on the same image Ryland saw. "*Crap...*" he let out, but Ryland didn't think he meant to. It spilled out so breathlessly and uneven in tone.

This entire time, there was a pickup truck tailing them. Its headlights were off and neither of the two could sort out its true color. It loomed over them like a monstrous shadow in the fast-approaching twilight. Charlie muttered something about it not being a brilliant idea to make sudden moves. He feared that doing so would raise an alarm to their stalker. Still, Ryland begged for him to do something. *Anything.* Charlie's grip tightened on the steering wheel, as Ryland watched the ones in his mind churn, weighing the risks that might potentially provoke their greatest fears.

With each passing moment, the tension mounted as it weighed over their head like a guillotine. Ryland squeezed her eyes shut, silently pleading for divine intervention. The pounding of her heart echoed like a nauseating drumbeat deafening her senses against the silence of the desert.

Finally, something in Charlie sparked a surge of determination, as Ryland watched him sprang forward. The engine roared to life with each acceleration, kicking up a billowing cloud of dust in their wake. The landscape blurred past them in a whirlwind of motion. The adrenaline-fueled rush drowned the fear threatening to consume them.

The race toward safety soon came to an inevitable halt as the call for speed tolerances forced them to slow down. Yet, their hearts did not. Their thunderous beatings blended with another, both disturbing the atmosphere of relief. The lights of the town flickered into view like a beacon of hope in the darkness, as Charlie eased off the accelerator. The couple remained quiet, even until reaching their hotel. Thankfully for Ryland, as they ducked inside the shelter of their room, the tension had finally dissipated like a storm passing overhead. They decided it was best to get some shut eye so they could run out of town first thing in the morning. For Ryland, however, the echoes of fear lingered, reminding her of the danger that lurked in the shadows, waiting to strike.

CHAPTER THREE

The night dragged on as Ryland hoped for daybreak. As soon as the sun rose, she and Charlie leaped out of bed, eager to pack their belongings and disappear down the road.

After checkout, Charlie checked the gas levels of his car but quickly kicked himself when he saw how low they were. "The stupid thing must've drained when we sped last night," Ryland heard him mutter to himself. That knocked her hopes down to size, meaning they would have to stay longer.

However, grace proved to be on their side as Charlie spotted a gas station on the outskirts of town. Before he left the car, he leaned over to Ryland, ensuring that she'd stay put. "Do not open the door for anyone," he warned. Ryland didn't need much reminding of that at all, considering her stomach was still in knots. Charlie slipped out of the driver's seat. Though he didn't dare venture forward until he was certain that all four doors were locked. Ryland cheered when he also left the car on to allow cool air to flow from the ventilator. It was like a kiss on her skin, despite having to sit in 90-degree temperatures. The day had not yet reached brunch hour.

As Charlie dove into the store, her eyes remained trained on him. She watched him briefly greet the store clerk with a spark of conversation. She hoped it was more about their need for gas. As if to answer her question, she saw Charlie hand over his debit card. A quiet cheer rose within her, not just for the promise of a full tank, but especially seeing Charlie return to her in one piece.

The driver's door swung open as the dark-haired beau poked his head inside. He flashed a gentle smile then quickly shut off the engine. It prompted a pout from Ryland, as she was shorthanded on the supply of good air. Noticing this, Charlie climbed in to kiss her head. "It'll be quick, I promise," he assured.

All Ryland could do was sit back and will herself to remain still. But the beads of sweat were more evident against every attempt to wipe them away. Her last attempt was accompanied with as many gulps of water as her stomach would allow. Inevitably, her best efforts fell apart as temperatures rose. Exhaustion started to seep in before she even had the chance to exert her energy on something more useful. Just as Charlie started pumping, Ryland's gaze spotted a familiar figure standing outside the store. She had an open magazine in one hand and, in the other, a glossy red lollipop. She sported the same dingy outfit as before, but this time, her hair was cut to her shoulders. Without realizing it, her limbs took on a mind of their own, causing her to slip out of the car. As she crossed over, Ryland waved slightly at the familiar face.

The girl noticed the crimson-haired darling as quickly as she was approached. She flashed a small grin, but her eyes were soaked in suspicion. "Hey..." the girl greeted casually.

"I'm not sure if you remember..." Ryland started. "We met back at the diner two nights ago. You also met my partner."

At first, the girl showed no hint of recognition. Then, out of the blue, her eyes lit with the same excitement from their first encounter. "Oh, right!" she exclaimed. Her gaze drifted to Charlie, whom Ryland realized was watching the entire time. He gave a curt nod, but emotions remained reserved behind the curious glint in his eye. Still, the girl rambled on. "So, y'all leavin' town?"

"I'm afraid so," Ryland responded, almost curtly.

The girl raised her thin dark brows. "Why so soon?" she questioned. "You just got here..."

Ryland nodded but her mind replayed her nightmares all over again. The shadows of the unexpected continued to taunt, although their voices were much louder last night, effectively disturbing her sleep. In the spur of her tug-a-war with reality, the girl's words broke through the noise in Ryland's mind and pitched a much more haunting tune. "We've spent all the time needed," Ryland noted.

"Not, when it's only been a day..." the girl refuted. The innocence in her stare was more unsettling to Ryland, blissfully unaware of what she just said.

Ryland decided it was best to stick with her first mind. A part of her knew it would disappoint Charlie. "I don't want to keep my partner waiting," she stated, liberally using him as an excuse for a speedy retreat. Before completely closing off, Ryland flashed a sweet smile and said something about it being pleasant to run into her again.

When she returned to Charlie, he immediately bombarded her about the encounter. But Ryland deflected by reminding him of the dwindling hours of daylight. Reluctantly on his part—but fortunately for her—he obliged and followed Ryland back to the car. "So, where to next?" she quizzed, as she slipped on her seatbelt.

Charlie shrugged as he searched through the notes app on his phone, where he stored a list of places to visit on the trip. Then his eyes shifted over to Ryland, with a grin dancing on his face. "How about Globe?" he pitched.

That was far enough for her.

The GPS led Charlie and Ryland onto a road with a backdrop of humming engines and streaks of gold and bright blue all around them. The windows were rolled down, allowing a gush of wind to blow their hair all over the place. With eyes fixed on the road, neither of the two noticed the recurrent brushing of their copper and ebony strands until they became entangled at one point. Then, shortly after the entangling, the copper and ebony slipped from each other's grasp and succumbed to the influence of the wind.

It had been nearly a half hour since they left Holbrook. In that span, they were given a moment of tranquility, enough to enjoy the consistent flow of the road. Moments like this were often fleeting in their relationship. It was a much-needed opportunity to enjoy each other in silence just for once. But a passing thought crossed Ryland's mind. She raised internal protest to preserve the peace she clenched onto, but the chime of her ringtone blared against the roars of the wind. It pulled her attention to her purse, which rested at her feet. Begrudgingly, she fished out her phone. The screen was already lit, revealing the caller ID.

It was her mother.

Ryland rolled up the windows as her thumb slid the green button a bit too soon. Before she let out a "Hello", she was bulldozed with incessant questioning.

"Where are you!" Mama demanded.

The call wasn't on speaker nor did the volume blare, but Charlie heard enough to flash wide eyes in her direction. "What is she going on about now?" he mouthed. He, too, experienced his fair share of Mama's insufferable temper. Ryland remembered when Charlie met Mama for the first time. It was eleven months into their relationship. The greeting led to a conversation about family, prompting Mama to relive the old days with her photo album. But the warm welcome quickly soured when Mama uncovered an image of a 22-year-old version of herself in a white gown and melancholy behind her eyes. Shortly after, the conversation deteriorated, adding more fuel to the already complicated relationship between the scarlet rose and her mother.

"It's been days, Ryland! Days!" she scolded. "No call... No text... Not one peep! I stopped by your apartment only to find more boxes everywhere, but *not you.*"

"I'm with Charlie," Ryland explained. "We needed a getaway."

Mama scoffed at her words. "So, you eloped?" she accused. "I knew it!"

"We didn't—"

"No wonder you're already moving in with the guy!"

Ryland lowered her arm, pulling the phone from her ear. Frustration swarmed inside her like a cloud of bees, while Mama was like a rage of wasps. The scarlet rose resorted to silence to cope with the rising lump in her throat. It wasn't tears, but the immense temptation to rip a hole in her mother. But it wasn't worth it. She was also weary of Charlie seeing her like that, even if he already had a glimpse. She feared the toxicity would give him cold feet. But judging his furrowed brow and clamped jaw put out the flames of panic rising within her. She was especially surprised to see him so willing to shoulder her burden.

Suddenly, she didn't feel so alone.

A forthwith of courage flushed out the anguish in her veins, coursing her thumb to slap the red button. Then she shut off her phone and tossed it back into her purse. But sooner than expected, she found herself drowning in shame all over again. She averted her gaze to the window, attempting to avoid having to face Charlie. Until she felt his hand rest on hers. The floodgates of her tear ducts opened, and out came seventeen years of pain silently rolling down her face.

"You think I don't get it?" Charlie finally spoke. "In a lot of ways, my parents and I were always like that. It got worse after my sister ran away. We did everything we could to understand each other, but eventually I accepted that we'd never see eye to eye."

"I don't want either of us to put our kids through that," Ryland heard herself say. "If you can't hold any vow, at least keep that." But as soon as those words slipped out, she was grappled with guilt that shocked her sober. Her head whipped in his direction, but it was too late. Her words had already sunk into him. "It's not that I think you won't—"

"It's fine," he cut her short. "I get it."

"I know you'll be great," she said, striving to save the moment. "I just... I want you to know that."

"It's my fear too," Charlie engaged, his eyes still fixed on the road. "I'm more afraid of losing a child."

Such rawness and candor was a punch in the gut. The scarlet rose desired to take every bit of Charlie in that moment and guard those pieces with her life. The avowed look in his eyes confessed the same.

The twosome spent the rest of that ride in something close to tranquility again. But emotions were still heavy, and uncertainties lingered like a black cloud, threatening to wreak havoc. The sun burned ten times hotter on their skin, and the brightness of the blue hues in the sky felt more ominous as the day dragged on.

CHAPTER FOUR

Her phone buzzed in her pocket again. That was the fifth time that night.

Adrenaline still pumped through her veins. Every burst from her racing heart felt like fire. Her cheeks were soaked from the tears still pouring from her eyes. She couldn't move in any clear direction, walking senselessly in circles. She must have walked around the street of their home for the umpteenth time. She couldn't go back inside, knowing that Mama was there.

The second rising lump in her throat had finally burst. It was another round of tears. Her salt-soaked lips parted beyond her control as her voice spilled from the opening. "You were happy for her!" she belted. "Why not me?" Her words carried into the night, but she couldn't have cared less if they reached Mama's ears. She crumpled to the floor, feeling like she was nothing more than a tossed piece of paper. For the first time, she had finally reached her breaking point. How could Mama think of her like that? She knew her mother wouldn't have taken it well. In a way, Ryland reasoned that it was a frightening revelation. She did break the number one rule—no men, career only. And so did Callie, her older sister. Ryland never understood why she couldn't have both. She burned for connection. So, the taste for affection brewed as the years went on. Somehow, she managed to stay grounded through high school and her first years of college with supplemental friendships. Until she met him.

Then again, she was never the favorite child but merely a golden goose of Mama's standards.

After a long while of emotions eating away her mind, Ryland decided it was time to swallow her pride and pull herself to her feet. She fingered through her hair, attempting to smooth out the knots. Then, shortly after straightening her clothes, she headed for her car. But induced into autopilot, her blood and bones animated her shock-riddled body. Somehow, in another given moment, she found herself standing on the porch steps with her head hanging low and desperately stabilizing a shaky finger hovering the doorbell.

Charlie's parents did well with money. Enough to dispose. But engulfed in a childhood saturated with riches instead of love, he was estranged by them. His sister's disappearance was the final straw. So, Charlie made a disappearance of his own when he left for college. This lasted for five years until his parents found him a year after his graduation. But this night was around the same time Ryland was left to her own devices, circulating through the streets until they led her to Charlie.

He found himself fighting to repel his parents' control over his home. The McCaulins couldn't fathom how he achieved so much on his own. His stability and prosperity shook them to the bone. It was confirmation of their profound ignorance all along—that they merely adopted him and his sister for self-glory. Their mask of reconciliation slipped as their underlying intentions swiftly showed face. That lonesomeness had seeped in tremendously, and their own three-story home had begun to attract moths of guilt eating away their conscience. But this only reignited the old flame of resentment burning rampant between the dark-haired beau and the McCaulins.

Before senses could pull either one back, he and his parents were sucked into a whirlwind of rage. Reaching the final straw, he almost walked out of his own house. He wanted to go anywhere but there. Until he saw her face at the door. Her name slipped from his lips in a chaotic blend of dismay and urgency. "What's wrong?" he questioned, hastily, with an arm reaching out for her.

"I can't go back home..." was all she could let out.

As soon as she said this, he gave up his frustrations and ushered her inside.

Ryland rode out three months before she finally found a place of her own. While under the wings of her fiancé in those three months, she found herself beholden by his tenderness. He agreed to hold off on their engagement until she was on her feet again. Still, those months were rocked by many trials with little breakthrough. Sometimes their hidden monsters reared their vicious heads at the slightest triggers. Those nights were the worst when she and Charlie went so long without a single word of truce. Even when they drifted back to one another, wounds lingered and scarred.

But darkness must surrender to the light eventually; and that *was* whenever those bleak orbs landed on Charlie. A sense of solace kissed her soul and returned a warmer hue of brown in her eyes. This same confidence flowered again as she followed every trace and spark in his gaze and tender hands on the wheel. When those deep sienna eyes found hers, she envisioned their future all over again, and each time was like the first.

Their journey so far had finally led them to Globe. It was a town of hidden gems and many mysteries that left the couple on their toes. Unsure of where to explore first, they took advantage of another pit stop to brainstorm. Ryland started to notice a pandemonium of impulsion brewing in their pre-honeymoon, soon only leaving room to heavily rely on instinct. The thought alone gave her butterflies, but a hidden part of her enjoyed every bit of such a mystery. For once, she didn't have to grasp at straws for something. She could just feel and simply be.

As she was perched on top of the car hood with legs crossed and her phone in hand, she scrolled through the options to visit. She lifted her eyes a bit, enough to catch Charlie, who leaned against the driver's door with his gaze astray, landing on nothing. Mindlessly, he munched on bits of a granola bar he grabbed from whatever was left of their batch of road treats. His long raven tresses had gradually shriveled into loose curls as they achieved a maroon shade in the sunlight. With his olive complexion baked evenly into a golden hue, Ryland always wondered how the heck he managed to keep his skin so smooth, as hers often got splotchy on the cheeks if left too long in the heat.

Ryland continued to let herself drink in his beauty against the desert backdrop. He sported a half-buttoned white shirt tucked into dark denim jeans while almost every finger on both hands was laced with bohemian rings. Most of all, he kept on his favorite chain—a gold cross—which rested so effortlessly on his sculpted chest. For Ryland, that necklace was a symbol of their shared faith. Whenever she was drawn to it, the scarlet rose wondered if the same appreciation crossed his mind.

She must've stared at him for too long because Charlie whipped his head in her direction. Her heart fluttered like pattering wings in her chest. Her bones rattled with glee as he glided toward her. He planted a kiss on her temple; as his lips were warm and soft against her skin. When he pulled away, his voice carried softly in her ears. "Did you find something you like?" he remarked.

Almost washed over with guilt, she thought he meant the way she stared at him. But a whisper pulled her eyes to the opened browser on her phone. That, and Charlie was not a high-hat, though he had a ritzy air about him. Equipped with such charisma, he pulled all sorts of attention from any girl who laid her eyes on him. But hold up a mirror and he'd never see the comely face staring back at him.

Moreover, as he spoke, he nodded his head in the direction of her phone in hand. "Oh... um..." she tried to answer but embarrassingly stumbled over her words as her thumb scattered up and down the webpage. She felt his bemused eyes on her with a possible smirk tugging on one cheek. "How about... a park?" she suggested.

Charlie shrugged it off. "We should save that for the end of our trip," he admitted. "I have something in mind I've been wanting to treat you to."

Instinctively, her brows arched. "Really?" she bantered.

He lowered his face to hers, close enough for their noses to barely touch. She found herself again a molten mess trapped in his gaze. How, after all this time, could he still make her dizzy? Finally, his voice broke through her thoughts as he replied, "Really..."

Given no chance to fire back, his hand slipped under hers. His eyes shifted to the brightened screen as she knew he was already memorizing the recommended list of hotspots to visit. Swiftly, the burdened task was taken on by Charlie. After another moment of glossing through the list, he turned to Ryland and asserted, "I got it sorted out."

That was all she needed to hear, enough to feel safe and follow his lead.

Another few miles brought them further into the desert. The sun had dipped low on Ryland's curiosity as Charlie eased his Silverado into the parking lot. Her head was on slow rotation as her eyes needled all she could humanly analyze. Everything beneath the falling sun was plagued with shadows casted across the land. Charlie announced their arrival with a chirpy steward-like voice. "We're here!"

His random moment of silliness disarmed her nerves almost instantly as an unintentional smile crept on her glossed lips. For a moment, her thoughts were silenced. Charlie wasted no time as he slipped out of the car and maneuvered to the other side, where he let Ryland out. As her feet met the gravel, a soft earthy incense in the air brushed against the walls of her lungs. The warmth of it on her exposed skin peeking out of her spaghetti tank top was just as soothing, but not more calming than Charlie's hand in hers as he guided them toward the ancient ruins.

Her eyes followed where the golden streams of the setting sun landed, which illuminated the beauty of the weathered landscape. "So, this is really where the Salado people lived?" Ryland remarked in awe.

"I'm sure it looked a lot more like a home in its heyday, but yes," Charlie responded as they inched closer to the pueblo complex.

They spent a long while wandering, carefully drinking in what the old bones of the American desert had to offer. There were a handful of rooms. Exploring each one eventually led them to what looked like the central plaza. They admired the remaining stonework that showcased the advancement of Besh Ba Gowah's ancient settlers. After some time, they found themselves approaching a kiva the Salado people used for ceremonies. Ryland and Charlie stepped through the low doorway, still hand in hand, although Ryland's attention was on her left as Charlie's was toward his right. They were met with a cool timbered scent that kicked up from the soil, stones, and twigs inside. For some reason, it was that moment where they felt the weight of the past. A tale of the centuries that was once lost in time.

"You know, there's still not much known about them," Charlie mentioned. "Other than how they were chased away from their home—thanks to a fickle climate."

Ryland found Charlie once again as he remained glued to their earthy surroundings. He started to babble like a professor half-talking to himself while staring at each artifact. To his knowledge, there were countless floods and droughts that depleted their resources. Eventually, the ancient settlers were forced to abandon their once fruitful home. Ryland couldn't tell what she loved most in that moment: the alluring lace of his words filling her ears or the flame she saw in his eyes that reminded her of their love language. To be intrinsically simulated. They could talk for hours about anything, especially the history that scaled around them.

Connecting in such a way was how they told each other, "I understand you".

She felt herself pulled into his embrace. It wasn't only his arms that did so, but the gravity between them they called love. Hearts locked and brown eyes pouring into one another so freely. And so, they sealed that promise of unity like a vow. Ryland felt compelled to their locked hands and was moved by the marquise diamond on her finger. "Their story sounds like ours, doesn't it?" spilled out of her lips. "Running from unstable homes. Trying to make a life of our own."

His hand slipped under chin and lifted her face to his. "*We* are our new home," he promised. "One with no floods or droughts. We'll be a hidden oasis—a treasure no one can find but us."

How perfect is that?

Still, the voices of Ryland's ghosts crept in.

Was it intuition or doubt?

CHAPTER FIVE

By the time Charlie and Ryland arrived at a hotel nearest to Miami, the sky had finally reached a dark velvet shade. Above their heads, the full moon danced in its silver glory like a floating mirrorball, and next to it were stars like diamonds sprinkled across the sky. The couple had cruised all the way to their destination, slowly taking in all the night had to offer.

Check-in, on the other hand, was a flash.

Charlie uttered their names to the clerk and showed ID in exchange for their key. As soon as the couple folded into their room, Charlie flopped on the bed while Ryland beelined for the balcony. They were on the fifth floor, so

Ryland was eager to continue gazing at the firmament above.

For the first time, her mind was at peace. The only thoughts she thumbed through were the memories accumulating since the start of their trip. Every touch, every soothing word, and the way Charlie cared for her left Ryland enraptured.

Then, two arms slipped around her waist as the familiar feeling of Charlie's chin rested on her shoulder. "I've always wanted to find an Ursa," he said. "I've been waiting to cross that off my bucket list."

The thought alone made Ryland chuckle. "You say that every time we catch a night like this," she teased. "For my sake, I hope that night comes sooner." Charlie laughed, but she meant it. Once a guy is whisked away with a newfound passion, his lover is doomed to hear about it at any given trigger. Ryland was convinced that she would be more relieved when Charlie finally found himself an Ursa. Either Major or Minor—it did not matter. She needed one to satisfy Charlie's on and off, but endless search. Admittedly, she was curious to find one too.

"Let a man dream..." he bantered, with his gaze glued to the cosmos that reflected in the pools of his eyes.

Ryland let her head rest against his. She could stay that way forever. But the vigorous echo of a growl erupting from her belly disturbed the stillness of the moment. *"Ugh, like clockwork!"* her mind scolded her stomach. She would have leapt from whatever she was doing to indulge and satisfy a craving. But not this time. Charlie's arms retracted from around her and, like the warmth between them, he slipped away. His absence incited goosebumps across her skin. Charlie mumbled something about ordering takeout while on his way off the balcony. Ryland didn't have much of a choice. So, she ducked inside after him. They spent a while bouncing back ideas: tacos, pizza, or maybe something from a diner that delivers. Suddenly, the taste for vegetable lo mein crept on her tongue until the thought of it was unavoidable, vexing another demanding growl from her insides.

"How about Chinese?" she suggested. Charlie was happy with that idea.

As the dark-haired beau detailed their order over the phone, Ryland rested in bed and began scrolling through her email inbox for the only priority that popped into mind: she needed to check who RSVP-ed to their wedding. So far, five more people have claimed their attendance. This meant that the current head count in total was about 27 people. She noted in mind that there was still legroom in their budget for a few more guests. In contemplating, she was provoked to the thought of her mother. She checked the names of the people, but they were just childhood friends and college buddies shared between Ryland and Charlie's list. Only three of those names were family members—Charlie's two cousins and Ryland's older sister.

Charlie must have sensed the shift in Ryland. No longer on the phone, he crawled on the bed and laid parallel to her. Like an exposed nerve under his scanning stare, she could no longer conceal the ghosts that haunted her glossy dark orbs. She wasn't taken by surprise when Charlie reached out to her. Warmth returned when his palm rested on her cheek. Her scarlett lashes fluttered as her lids squeezed shut, behaving like a last standing gate against the invasive force of salt-soaked regret. Charlie did not prob nor prod, but instead conjured up ways to guide her back into the present.

Gosh, he had such a way of doing that. "What do you think I most appreciate about you?" flowed from his lips so effortlessly. His words were like the pouring of honey in her ears and hyssop to her plagued heart.

Her eyes twitched at the gentle husk of his voice, as her gaze found Charlie once again. The desire to be treasured always seemed to be a child's wish. But she attempted to search deep. The question rolled over again and again within the walls of her mind. Despite such effort, she came up short of a suitable answer. All she could do was shrug.

Charlie didn't scoff or pity her. The look on his face was evident and assuring that not one thought was raised against her. "You're so earnest," he said. "Everything about you runs so deep. I always know where we stand—even when things get muddy—because, with you, everything just clicks."

Just like that, tears spilled forth. A chuckle escaped her, though it was tinged with melancholy. "Is it safe to say that you're everything I ever wanted?" she heard herself say.

His face pulled back with a glint dancing in his eyes as he rolled them. "I'd say there's still room for improvement," he mocked at himself, causing Ryland's chest to rattle profoundly with laughter.

"Maybe..." she teased back. "I'm not afraid of a challenge."

Charlie's eyes softened and so did his smile. His hand never left Ryland's face. He inched closer, enough for the depths of their deep brown pools to spill into one another. "What made my dove so sad?" he cooed. "Did we have a rough day?"

Ryland shook her head. "Today was my favorite," she assured him. Tender confusion blanketed Charlie's face until she revealed the list of attendees on her phone. She watched him rifle through the names and sorted out his reaction to each one his eyes landed on. Gradually, an unmistakable sunken look settled in. Then, he peered up at her. "I'm starting to think hanging on to that kind of hope is no good for me," she added, plainly.

Then she was pulled into Charlie's arms, her tears already pouring down his shoulder. But he didn't flinch nor budge at a drop. "For what it's worth," he started to say, "I sent my parents an invitation. They're not coming either." As Ryland leaned back just enough to meet him at eye-level, he concluded, "I think it's best that way. I guess I'm just over everything with them."

At first, Ryland wondered how he could say such a thing. Who wouldn't want family by their side as they enter a new stage so life changing as marriage? Most couples wanted that. *She wanted that.* But while the urge to rebuttal grew strong on her tongue like the taste of poison, a saving thought stifled any opportunity. Was it worth it? To have one moment of forged happiness only to come out of it with new scars that might last an eternity? Suddenly, images played over her eyes. She could see disgruntled stares knifing out the pleasantry of walking down the aisle, and the snide whispers from across the table sounded so real.

As they were on the verge of voicing their thoughts, the jarring vibrations of Charlie's phone jolted them out of their minds. Now it was his turn to despise an interruption, as a wince slipped from his lips.

Reluctantly, he peeled himself off the bed and grabbed his phone from the nightstand on his end. "Hello?" he answered. Ryland sat up too, watching every twitch of his muscle when he recognized the caller. "Oh! Sure... I'll be down in a sec. Thank you!" Ryland was ready to question him, but he told her, "Our delivery is downstairs. I'll be back."

Ryland simply nodded. She remained where she was until Charlie ducked out of their room and disappeared behind the closing door. Then, she too rolled out of bed. She didn't have a specific goal, but any would be a good enough distraction. She settled on the idea of washing her face since her cheeks started to feel sticky with tear stains. She grabbed her travel-size face cleansers from her suitcase, then beelined for the bathroom. Ryland stole a glance of her reflection in the sink mirror. Her complexion was flushed with a faded trail of mascara lining across her skin, and her still soaked lashes had started to resemble spider legs. Her untouched lip gloss was the only sight intact. She scoffed as soon as her sights landed on them. Charlie had once pointed out how he never met a girl whose lipstick or gloss never smudged after a meal. As a foodie, she had to master the art of lipwear.

She took advantage of roughly five minutes or so to wash off her ruined makeup. When she came back up, she felt like a new person with a fresh face. As a finishing touch, she gently rubbed in some night cream as balm for her somewhat still flushed complexion. Charlie always reminded her of his love for their rosy hue and often expressed his affection with a peck. It was almost like he kissed her insecurity away.

As Ryland headed back into their room, she asked Charlie, "How did the food turn out?" She hadn't bothered to look his way until she was met with silence. *Utter silence.* Her mind erased the task of packing away her cleanser kit as her focus redirected on her now missing fiancé. "Charlie?" she called out. Her eyes scanned corner to corner, but he was nowhere to be found.

Ryland reached for her suitcase once again. This time to yank out a black hoodie. Her shorts were also replaced with a dark pair of jeans. Then, she pulled her long scarlet curls into a tight bun before heading for the door.

Outside of their hotel room were two ways to get to the lobby: the elevator and the stairway. Ryland wanted to use the elevator, but she was weary of the queue. So, she opted for the stairs. With her 5'6 sleek physique accustomed to jogging and cardio dancing, Ryland raced down the flights of stairs until she encountered the lobby entrance. As soon as she slipped through, she marched her way to the double glass doors leading out into the abyss of the night. She scanned the lobby on her way out but, again, no Charlie. As she started to leave the hotel, her sights spotted something alarming masked by the poorly lit darkness. She managed to make out a truck about a yard away in the parking lot. Nerves crept in all over again like phantom whispers screaming loud in her head. All she could think at that moment was: *Where is Charlie?*

At first Ryland did not see Charlie anywhere near the hotel front until a familiar voice broke through her festering nerves. She followed the voice until she found the only face that stilled her. *"Charlie!"* her mind chirped. Her footsteps quickened as his voice grew more audible.

Apparently, he wasn't that far from her at all. He was on the opposite end of the parking lot, standing near a sign that prompted a space for delivery drivers to use for drop-offs. Although overwhelmed with relief, she was quickly befuddled by something else.

There was no delivery driver.

Charlie was already holding a takeout bag. So why was he still out here? That's when something else snatched Ryland's attention. With eyes widened and mouth agape, her mind hissed, *"What is she doing here!"*

Were they being followed?

CHAPTER SIX

This time she didn't have a lollipop in her hand. Her chopped dark hair was no longer a tangled mess, but seemingly tidied with a straightener. She replaced her rugged clothes for an off-shoulder top that hugged her torso and high-waisted skinny jeans. But those scanning green eyes were very familiar and still spacey. As Ryland inched forward, she overheard the girl say, "You and your fiancée will love it! I promise!"

"What will I love?" Ryland inserted. She flashed a look at Charlie but slapped on a polite grin for the sake of making peace. Still, her eyes never ceased darting from the chatty duo to the truck hovering nearby. With another glance over her shoulder, her heart dropped to her feet. There was a silhouette dancing in the shadows behind the wheel, but the tinted windows blocked Ryland's view.

"Oh, hey!" Charlie greeted without a hint of skepticism in his voice. "Sabrina was telling me about a ranch nearby that we should try. It sounds like something you'd like."

Ryland's attention whipped back to her fiancé and the girl. "Sabrina?" she repeated.

The girl lifted a hand and gave a small wave. "Hi!" she clarified.

Ryland maintained her smile, but didn't hold back from saying, "It must be a small world for us to keep running into each other."

Sabrina laughed and agreed, but the meaning in Ryland's words was entirely different. "It's actually a good thing because I heard you two will be leaving town in the morning," she mentioned. "I didn't want ya to miss Veiled Heartstone Valley. It's loads o'fun!"

"It's the ranch she mentioned," Charlie clarified. "Apparently, it's something meant for couples. They have horseback riding, archery, workshops... Plus, the food options!" His brows wiggled at that last sentence.

Once again disarmed by Charlie, a giggle escaped Ryland against her will. She even felt her eyes twinkle until they traveled back to Sabrina. "It does sound like something I'd want to do..." she commented.

"Definitely, think on it," Sabrina nudged.

Charlie flashed her a grateful smile and said, "We will." Fortunately for Ryland, he wrapped up the conversation and ushered them back to their room.

On the way upstairs, Ryland wrestled with herself about this encounter. Sabrina seemed like a nice girl, but something about her genuinely spooked Ryland. On the other hand, she didn't want to upset Charlie with possibly imaginary assumptions.

Yet, as they neared their door, something hanging on it was all but imaginary. Taped on the surface was a new red string! "You've got to be kidding me!" she blurted out.

"What?" Charlie responded, frozen mid-inserting their key card in the slot. He followed her gaze to the string. At first, his countenance was blasé, as he remained undiscerning. Then it quickly hardened into something unreadable. He shifted his head about, his eyes darting everywhere, looking for more strings on other doors.

Much to Ryland's disappointment, there were none.

So, Charlie quickly opened their door, and hurried them inside. Ryland watched him take a moment to double check the security of their lock. He jingled the doorknob about three times before looking back at

Ryland in a way that gave her much relief. It was then that she realized the tension deepened in her neck and shoulders. As she stretched them out, the dark-haired beau flew to her side, landing on his knees as she was seated on the edge of the bed.

Once she sorted out the knots in her muscles, Ryland let her arms drop. Then she arrowed a glare at Charlie. "Don't ever scare me like that again," she scolded.

But her words confounded him. "What?"

"I thought you went *missing*," she told him.

Charlie planted his hand on her arm and flashed a reassuring grin. "I'm fine now, aren't I?"

Ryland rolled her eyes as she felt her cheeks grow hot. "Whatever..." she mumbled, looking elsewhere.

Charlie gave her one last squeeze before climbing to his feet and beelining for the takeout bag. He wiggled it in the air and said, "I hope you didn't lose your appetite."

Ryland opened her mouth to protest, as she was still rocked with nerves. But her stomach interrupted. A knowing smirk pulled on Charlie's face as he busied himself with the task of fixing their plates. Ryland watched his every move intently, but her mind started to pull her into some other place. She mulled over every possible speculation about the strings and the truck sightings she dared not mention to Charlie. It was then that she started losing heart about their trip. She just wanted to go home.

Instead, she spent the rest of the night in the dark about everything as usual. Unsure of which turn to take and who to do it with. To be haunted by uncertainty was torment in itself; and at that point, she hoped for anything to pull her out. All she wanted was some answers, or at least an escape.

"On second thought, dove, we might want to rethink this one," prompted Charlie.

He and Ryland were at a quick stop in the late morning, about 10 miles from the hotel they stayed in. Charlie had parked the car on the side of the road to focus on a blurb about the ranch on its website. As he searched for more information, Ryland was busy filtering through emails, recalculating the head count for their wedding.

Ryland peered up from her phone and darted a confused look his way. She was sitting on the roof as he leaned against the hood. From her point of view, she only caught the side of his sharp jawline and squinted eyes against the sun glare bouncing off his phone screen.

"What are you talking about?" she probed him, yielding his attention to her.

"Uh... *Veiled Heartstone Valley*..." he reminded her.

"Oh..." was her response as realization gradually trickled in. "What's wrong?" she asked him. "I thought it'd be fun for us."

At first, he didn't reply. His eyes dropped back down at his phone screen in hand. He scrolled through more webpages but ended up shaking his head as if he was fighting his own mind. "That was my initial thought," he finally said. "Until I'm learning that it's some therapy place in the middle of nowhere."

Ryland did think it was weird for a perfect stranger who knew nothing about their relationship to recommend therapy. On the other hand, there was room for misconception in translation. Deep inside, Ryland wasn't against the thought of trying out couple's therapy, especially with everything they've dealt with before and during their relationship. "I don't mind," she said. "It might help us."

Charlie lifted a brow. "Really?" he challenged.

"*Yes, really,*" Ryland shot back.

"This place is for people *on the brink of divorce!*" he explained, waving his phone in the air. "This is *not* a good idea for us."

Ryland straightened her back, bracing for a fight she saw coming. "Why not?" she pressed. "I'm a child of divorce and I don't want that happening to us or our kids, *if we have any*. Lest, you're on the fence about that and I didn't know about it."

"Ryland, that's not even fair to say!" her fiancé refuted. "You know, I want kids. I'm saying that joining this group might run the risk of planting seeds we don't need in our relationship. It's already loaded as it is."

"Exactly, my point!" Ryland stated. "I love you, Charlie, but this trip we're doing will not erase the fact that our relationship needs some saving."

Charlie scoffed as he straightened up and fully turned around to face her. "I'm sorry," he said, crudely. "I didn't notice our relationship failing."

That was like a blow to the gut, leaving Ryland winded. She took a step back in her mind, wondering how they ended up in that moment.

Out loud, she said, "There's nothing wrong with getting help. That doesn't mean you're failing. *Failing* is not getting help at all when there are clear rough spots that need sorting out. That's all I'm saying."

Still, she cowered at the sight of the wheels spinning in his mind, struggling to make sense of his thoughts—and hers. "This isn't the first time you brought up therapy," he admitted.

Their voices somehow recovered the calmness between them. But fear and distrust remained prevalent with the young couple still shakened. Charlie lifted his face to the sky, as if begging for intervention from a source on high.

Her stomach knotted as guilt weighed on her heart. *"What am I saying?"* she scolded herself. Riddled with disappointment, she said to him, "I didn't mean to upset you." She paused for a moment, her fingers tugging the root of her curls. After contemplating some more, she finally spoke up again. "But what if it wasn't by chance we kept running into Sabrina?"

Charlie shook his head. "We'll get past it all," he assured. His knuckles were white with his fingers clenched tightly around the edges of his phone. With the help of the sun beating against his cheeks, she could see heavy gloss in his eyes sparkling in its golden rays. She noticed then that his enriched bisque complexion was now drained of any saturation. The brown in his eyes—though once adrenalized—was smothered with bargain. It was clear to Ryland that he saw more than what his lips were willing to tell.

Her heart shattered as a thought she knew was true popped into mind. "How long have they been separated?" It was a question she wanted him to answer, but his silence and the tear rolling down his cheek spoke louder.

She had just punctured a layer of Charlie she had never known until then. "It's so strange to care about them as much as I do," he admitted. "They're not even my real parents."

Ryland fumbled for the right thing to say. But the more she tried, none stood worthy than simply uttering, "I'm sorry."

Her gentle-hearted beau peered up with eyes so tender. "I'm sorry," he said, earnestly. Then he paused in his tracks. But she saw his mind still juggling with the way his lower lip was tucked between his teeth and his gaze slowly drifting off.

The moment dragged as he stayed chained to his thoughts, until something had finally yanked him back. His next words were seemingly almost out of the blue as he said, "Maybe you're right... If it's something you want to do, then we'll give it a shot." Then he whipped around with a solemn look locked on face. "Only on the condition that if this turns out to be *a huge mistake*, we will leave. I'll drag you by the hand, if I have to."

Ryland slowly nodded, letting his pact sync in. "Okay..." she agreed. Internally, she prayed for a miracle.

The couple folded back into their Silverado and headed down the road. Neither of the two were sure of what to expect as they followed the directions guided by their GPS. As a glimpse of the sky and the bronze lands whipped by, the drive started to feel like whiplash. The last sign of life was a few miles back by the time the day reached high noon.

The highway stretched out ahead, cutting through the endless expanse of the desert. As they ventured forth, the vibrant scenery of the town they left behind slowly depleted into a muted palette of the desert beneath the vast blue skies. There were occasional splashes of green like cacti and patches of bushes embedded in the sun-kissed ground. It was like they were trapped in a dome of blue that made life suddenly feel so insignificant. They zoomed by rugged rock with surfaces mercilessly battered by the winds overtime.

Further along, what was left of the road gave way to a rougher path. Dirt kicked up clouds of dust behind them, swirling in the air before settling back to the earth. Ryland and Charlie found themselves surrounded by nothing but open land with bleached trees scattered about. Just as the GPS on the dashboard started to flicker, their senses were shocked by the sudden outburst of pastures all about them. It was like a signal of purposeful borders between reality and another dimension.

For a moment, Ryland almost forgot that they were just in the desert moments ago. She stole a glance at Charlie, who carefully guided the car through a narrow pathway that started to show obvious signs of erosion. Tingles of joy sparked her nerves as soon as her eyes laid on the endless view of horses and cabin-style homes. But her excitement was smothered by something unreadable written across Charlie's face. "Well, we made it..." she quipped, attempting to break the hair-raising silence between them.

"Mm hmm," was his response.

She hated it. Ryland wanted to call him out, but a strong part of her was willing to bargain for his favor again. Instead, she shifted her attention to the images of promises slowly sifting past their windows. The pair went on like that for what felt like eternity to Ryland. Until the car came to a halt. Ryland whipped her head in Charlie's direction, but he was baffled too.

Standing boldly on the outside of their windshield was a sign that read:

No Vehicles Beyond This Point

Past the sign was nothing but grass spreading beyond yonder. Standing in the way of the horizons were blurs of mountains established in their glory. Ryland immediately looked down at her bare legs exposed by the beige denim shorts and the caramel ballerina sandals on her feet. "I need to change," she said aloud but more to herself.

As she and Charlie stepped out of the car, his eyes darted everywhere, scanning the grounds for any sign of life besides the occasional horse sightings. Once Ryland reached the trunk, she unzipped her suitcase and sorted through her clothing until she found a modest pair of jeans. She quickly plucked them out, along with her favorite pair of high-top vans. She thought their soft blue color would maintain the breezy indie style of her faded white concert t-shirt. After closing the trunk, she took her chosen items to the backseat of their Silverado and changed there, which only took a few minutes.

As Ryland hopped back out of the car, Charlie perked up at the sight of her. "Are you all set?" he said in a brighter tone. Ryland was thrown off. Raising a brow, Charlie asked, "What is it?" Then his eyes widened a bit. "Is there something behind me?"

Shaking her head, she inched closer to him, carefully analyzing his face. "I just thought we still weren't okay," she finally told him.

Charlie paused in his tracks, for a moment, as if he was just noticing her for the first time. She let herself stay under the spotlight of his gaze. He closed the space between them and slipped his hand in the back of her neck. She felt herself pulled into his embrace and, honestly, it was what she needed. He looked her dead in the eyes and said, "I'm okay so long as you are okay."

Ryland nodded, happy to hear his voice in her ears. It didn't matter what he said. "I'm okay."

Charlie flashed a sweet smile, small and delicate.

The conversation died between them, but they didn't lose each other in silence. Ryland withdrew from Charlie for a bit and turned her attention back to their surroundings. She gazed at the voyage beyond the grass awaiting them, as her mind conjured up theories of what may be in store for them.

"Do you want to keep going?" Charlie asked her.

Something in Ryland started to shy away from the idea but she fought against it. "Let's go," she said, determinedly.

And so, they went.

CHAPTER SEVEN

Ryland and Charlie took their time walking across the fields. Each careful step led them closer to a possible sign in the right direction. Along the way, they quieted their nerves with random selfies and pictures of the scenery around them. With all that time of walking, signs of human life had finally appeared.

At first it was a brief hello with a person or two. Then their further venture led to more encounters with cliques here and there until they came across a full-blown community. Though they were all different faces, these people shared a similar look. The couple first noted the attire: mostly flannel, sundresses, and riding gear but everyone wore the same brown boots that barely scraped the knees. Because of the sweltering air, Charlie and Ryland wrote off their clothing choices as something to accommodate the ranch lifestyle. Somewhere among those sightings, they encountered some architecture. First the cabins they saw earlier, then larger structures that seemed more fit for communal uses.

The couple came across a structure that resembled a church house. A small set of steps led to two twin mahogany doors, and standing at the very top landing was a late middle-aged couple. The man had sandy hair, which showed signs of a salt and pepper hue. His dark blue eyes felt slightly withdrawn, as if the wheels in his mind had awakened. Yet, he wore a rustic elegance to him. Especially with the way the sage green of his linen shirt matched his peachy complexion, and how his arms were carelessly exposed from his rolled-up sleeves. As he lifted a limb to wave at the approaching younger couple, the fabric danced slightly with each movement. IIis style was completed with a dark pair of well-fitted chino and a solid leather belt with a silver bull head for a buckle. His boots were also leather with sturdy soles, yet the weathered material gave him a relatable appeal. However, it seems that his youthful streak was more pronounced with the woman by his side. She had flowy straight midnight tresses and round jewel green eyes. The cotton material of her soft baby yellow dress, which barely touched her knees, swayed melodically in the tame winds. A thick and transparent brown headband brushed back all strands of her hair with one clean sweep. She flashed a glossy smile, which felt like warmth to Ryland. The blushing beauty was especially taken back by the woman because of a familiar aura tied around her, but Ryland could not put her finger on it.

"Well, look what we got here!" the older man remarked. "Two bright faces have graced us today. How are y'all doing?"

Ryland grinned, demurely. She peered up at Charlie, who thankfully took the lead without needing to look her way. "Hi, I'm Charlie," he introduced. Then, glancing down at her, he added, "This is my fiancée."

The scarlet rose gave a quick wave and tried to match his confidence, but the tone in her face fell short. "Hi... I'm Ryland..."

"Charlie and Ryland... interesting name you got there..." said the older gentleman. He pressed a hand on his chest and said, "I'm Maxwell." Then, he wrapped his arm around the woman next to him and mentioned, "This is my wife, Sherrie."

Recognition sparked in Charlie's eyes, which Ryland marveled at how quickly they came to life. "Maxwell and Sherrie Turner?" he repeated. "As in the Turners who founded this ranch?"

Something ignited in their eyes but neither of the younger couple understood it. "We are!" Sherrie confirmed. "Founded back in 2011, and still going strong!"

"Assuming you read our site," Maxwell jumped in, "I take it you two are looking to join our group."

Ryland opened her mouth to tell him how much she wanted to but Charlie clarified, "We want to see if it is something that would work out for us."

Maxwell scoffed, while the friendly look on Sherrie's face didn't glitch. "Of course, it will, darling," she cooed. She nodded at the people all over the ranch. "Take some time to listen to their stories. Trust me, once you get a full look around, you'll want to try out a few sessions."

Maxwell flashed a smirk at his wife. "Well, honey, you know how us boys are," he lectured playfully. Looking back at Charlie, he added, "We're not very good at asking for help. Isn't that right, son?"

Even Ryland noticed that the grin on her fiancé's face had finally started to strain. "I'm all for therapy," he counteracted.

Then Charlie tried to voice some other thoughts, but the Turners were quicker. The older couple went the extra mile to pull him and Ryland into a mini tour. They blended the love of horses and nature with counseling practices that help revive relationships. Ryland had tried questioning which techniques they use, hoping that she might be able to replicate them in her own practice one day. Her question was immediately met with a whim of terms thrown at her like "solution-focused" and "the Gottman method". But once Ryland heard that the imago relationship method was also used, she almost felt sold.

"So how many couples have benefited from I-R-T?" she inquired, specifically to Sherrie. The more Sherrie talked, the more Ryland felt drawn to her. So much so that no one noticed Charlie's struggle to keep up.

"You'd be surprised," Sherrie answered. "Many of the couples that come here tend to have childhood trauma. Every time I've used that method, I've watched light spark in those eyes. Next thing you know, those couples flourish."

As the foursome approached a structure resembling a modest cottage home, Maxwell walked ahead to pause the tour. "Right now, a session is about to start," he explained. "If you like, I'd be happy to let you join and see how it fits."

"We also have sessions separate for men and women," Sherrie included. "You've just missed those since they are typically scheduled in the afternoon. If you stay for tonight, you are more than welcome to join those tomorrow."

Again, Ryland was ready to voice her approval. But something made her think twice. Though she was now in the arms of Sherrie, she glanced back at Charlie. He stared back blankly but Ryland did catch something in his gaze. That familiar but oh-so-hated feeling of distance reappeared like a monster emerging from the shadows. Just as Ryland called out to him, he once again threw her off. "Let's try it," he agreed.

Hit with such bewilderment, she almost felt her brows touch her hairline. "Really?" she gasped.

Instead of giving her an answer, Charlie turned to Maxwell and Sherrie. "What are we waiting for?" It drove Ryland up the wall that she could not figure him out. His readability was one of the things she needed in him. It's why she often felt safe with him no matter where they ventured off. She decided within herself to lean on the thought that he would finally open up when it was just the two of them. With that hope alone, she went with the flow and ducked inside the cottage building with the others.

In the heart of the rustic cottage was a group of twenty sat on the floor in a circle, all uniformed in posture. As the foursome walked in, all twenty pairs of eyes synchronously floated in their direction. Their blank faces switched to life, but Maxwell lifted his hands in the air, as if to hush their immediate queries without anyone uttering a single word. His smile widened and the blue in his eyes brightened as they danced around the room, taking in all the gazes welcoming him back in so quickly.

"Good evening, my friends!" he finally addressed them.

"Good evening!" chorused the group.

Like the people they saw on their way into the ranch, these individuals resembled the same fashion. They wore linen shirts ranging from shades of beige, olive, and rust with some sprinkles of darker colors like navy and black. Like Maxwell, their shirts were rolled at the sleeves and tucked into well-fitted jeans. Unlike him, however, their pants were held up with braided cloth belts and their boots looked more worn down than Maxwell's. On every left-hand wrist was a bracelet made of beads with a chunk of the dark-colored strings exposed. Each of the beads had letters on them. Even Ryland's 20/20 vision could not make out any words on them.

"It looks like attendance is perfect today," Maxwell commented, his voice disrupting her thoughts. "We were a bit off this week, but let's keep up attendance from now on." Then, he stepped back a bit to nudge the young couple up front, but the pair was quickly split with him in the middle. "These two decided to join a session with us," he informed the group. "They are soon to be wedded, so let's not scare them off the idea of marriage just yet." He said that last part as a joke, and everyone laughed. But neither Ryland or Charlie was fond of his comment. The scarlet rose quickly looked at Charlie, hoping that remark was not counted as a strike. Again, she was greeted with another confusing expression on his face as he remained glued to the group in front of him. "Everyone, please welcome Ryland and Charlie!" Maxwell instructed the group, as if he was a principal addressing a classroom of school in need of direction.

And the group did as they were told. "Good evening, Ryland and Charlie!"

Even the red-haired darling cringed at the sound of her name in their mouths. The room's only light source was the setting sun streaming through the windows and some lanterns hanging from the corners of the walls. Her senses heightened with chills slicing up her spine, although she quickly wrote them off as nerves. So, she flashed a honeyed grin and waved at the unknown faces. Charlie's greeting was curt with a small wave and a silent nod.

Ryland took the lead and guided the pair to a spot in the back of the room, ensuring they sat next to each other. Though, she felt more comfortable nearest to the sunlit windows. Charlie slipped his hand in hers, interlacing their fingers. Ryland gazed up at him, as her doubts washed away. At least for that moment.

Sherrie and Maxwell took their places, as well, and began to lead the session.

Now within the circle, the unfamiliar faces surrounding them seemed more human. Ryland noticed a couple across from her and Charlie. They appeared no older than their mid-thirties at best. The woman's fading ash-brown hair showed signs of aging, but her deep-set, mercury-colored eyes resembled a silver sea of vigilance. Her shoulders were angled toward the man beside her, who sported a crew cut and a clean goatee. The woman's plain lips were slightly parted as her gaze fixated on the man. It was as though she counted every moment spent with him. The man, however, faced away from her, his stare downcast. Something more pressing had his attention.

Ryland's analyzing orbs shifted to another couple. They seemed closer to her and Charlie's age and possibly their background. Ryland was taken by the young woman's beauty, her lavender hair spilling over one shoulder. Thick lashes framed her monolid eyes as she remained fixated on her partner. Unlike the previous couple, this man reciprocated her attention. Ryland admired how engaged they seemed. Every now and then, a silent chuckle brightened the young woman's features, her partner's cheeks flushing in response. *What are they doing here?* Ryland wondered. But that question turned inward as she glanced at Charlie's hand in hers. She almost asked herself the same.

Sherrie's voice broke her thoughts. "Typically, we'd start our sessions with updates on how far we've come," she explained. "But for the sake of our newcomers, let's share our stories as a bit of encouragement." At the thought alone, Ryland's heart was soon a mess of sporadic flutters. Her eyes swiftly darted to Charlie. Instead of finding comfort in his protective gaze, his attention remained on the Turners.

The aging brunette spoke up, gaining immediate approval from Maxwell and Sherrie. "Lydia!" Maxwell cheered. "Your and Adam's story would be perfect for those still deciding to join us!"

Lydia smiled contentedly before sweeping her gaze across the room, lingering on the young couple. As Lydia began her story, the Turners sat back like directors satisfied with the performance unfolding. Maxwell clasped his hands, his blue eyes intense. Sherrie leaned forward with one shoulder pressing against her husband's.

"Adam and I have been married for sixteen years," Lydia began. "I barely made it through school, even with government assistance, and already had my first daughter by seventeen. Adam grew up in a low-income home, so he couldn't finish high school. He took on the best jobs he could find until he joined the military at eighteen." Her husband, Adam, nodded along as the layers of their past unraveled, though his head hung lower with each detail. "While he was still in the reserves, we got married at nineteen. Our marriage started off beautifully, despite the financial struggles. But by the time our first son was born, Adam got deployed, and our marriage went BANG!" She slapped her knee, sending shock waves across the room and earning herself a few flinched faces. "I felt alone as Adam, consumed by the need to build our finances, became distant. He wasn't there anymore, and neither was I. Eventually, we found stability, but our marriage remained in shambles."

Ryland's heart softened with every word. The cracks in Lydia's voice drew her in. Even Charlie shifted in himself, if only briefly. "It wasn't until we found Heartstone and met Sherrie and Maxwell that our marriage was saved," Lydia continued. "Adam and I fell in love all over again. Now, we take things step by step."

"Yes, Lydia, sometimes that's all we can do," Maxwell interjected. He turned to the group. "We get so caught up in climbing life's ladders—whether for finances, love, career, or family. We consume ideology after ideology to cope with our broken worlds, instead of healing the wounds we try to conceal with compensation."

"Thank you for sharing, Lydia," Sherrie said warmly. "You and Adam have shown so much bravery, facing these inner challenges head-on. True change begins with willingness."

Maxwell shot Sherrie a pleased look before moving on to the next couple.

Everyone's attention shifted to the young woman with lavender hair and her partner. The man spoke first. "Hi, I'm Xavier," he said, ruffling his natural onyx-colored hair, streaked with blonde. When he turned briefly toward the Turners, Ryland noticed a small hole in his nose where a ring had likely been removed. "It's been quite a journey for us too. Thanks to *these two*, Cheyenne and I have grown closer than ever."

"You two are on your way to replacing Max and me as the golden couple here!" Sherrie teased. The group let out short-lived laughter, but Ryland noticed something flash across Maxwell's face.

"No, no, no!" Cheyenne exclaimed, her voice bubbly but rattled with nerves. "We could never!"

Xavier continued their story. "We're high school sweethearts, but not because we're both Korean American. We've faced a lot of stigmas over the years. Now, at 27, we're engaged to be married in December. But as we got closer to marriage, I started developing severe anxiety. I want to be a good husband and a present father, especially since I never knew mine. Cheyenne's parents have been married for nearly 30 years, and we want to follow in their footsteps."

"We recently celebrated their anniversary," Cheyenne added. "That's a goal for us: to have a long, happy life together."

"Perfection is a dangerous doctrine we often adopt without realizing it," Maxwell said, leaning back, his fingertips pressed together. "In a society obsessed with appearing put together, we hide behind masks, never allowing ourselves the safety to truly heal. That false identity blocks our journey to self-actualization."

Ryland nodded along, reflecting on his words. *Have Charlie and I ever been that honest with each other?*

She thought about the vulnerable moments they had shared, but now wondered how much of their true selves had been uncovered. Charlie's expression, on the other hand, remained unreadable, though she noted the tension in his clenched jaw.

As if sensing the shift, Sherrie turned to them. "Ryland, Charlie, how are you finding things here?"

Ryland straightened upright, startled by the direct question. When she glanced back at the group, the once familiar faces now seemed distant and strange. "It's... different."

Sherrie grinned, but her eyes narrowed slightly, assessing Ryland. "I understand. Healing often requires stepping into the unknown. It's facing discomfort, and releasing the fear of change. It can be painful, but the journey is always beautiful."

Ryland allowed herself to smile, but it felt shifty under Sherrie's scrutinizing gaze. The tension between her and Charlie persisted. Charlie, his voice low and unwavering, broke the silence. "What if pain isn't just about growth, but something... darker?"

A heavy stillness settled over the group as Charlie's words hung in the air. Maxwell's gaze sharpened. "That's fear talking, son," he said, his tone stern, almost paternal. "Looking within can disturb the false sense of self we've built."

Ryland's insides knotted up at Maxwell's pointed response, as a growing dissonance gnawed at the back of her mind. Was Charlie afraid? Was she?

Charlie maintained Maxwell's gaze. "No," he replied coolly. "I just think calling it a 'mask' oversimplifies things. Some people wear masks, sure. But most people wear bandages. Would you walk around with an open wound?"

Maxwell leaned forward. "It's about trusting the healing process, not clinging to the pain," he retorted. "We'll explore that more in future sessions."

Ryland could see temptation in Charlie's eyes, but, thankfully for her, he opted for silence. Ryland refocused on the group as the discomfort gradually ebbed. The rest of the session carried out with more couples stepping forward with their stories—some inspiring, others tearful. Ryland found herself moved by the experience, but a nagging doubt persisted, creating a growing rift between herself and everything around her.

As the session came to a close, Sherrie clapped enthusiastically. "Beautiful, everyone! Remember, *every step is progress.*"

As the group slowly dispersed, Ryland turned to Charlie, whispering, "What was that about?"

Charlie blinked in response as he was confused at first. Then he glanced at the now-emptying circle. When his gaze returned to her, his eyes were heavy with thoughts swirling behind them. "I need you to know that I trust us," he aimed.

Ryland bit her lip, as his words would stand to haunt her for a time.

CHAPTER EIGHT

As Ryland and Charlie stepped outside, they were met with fresh air that kissed their exposed skin and the expectant faces of the Turners. As the warm breeze swept across the open land, a faint earthy scent was like a sweet fragrance. The sky had finally dimmed into a velvety color, and the celestial bodies which reigned the night were once again a shimmering kaleidoscope in Ryland's eyes. The ranch was now bathed in twilight, which gave the scarlet rose a renewed sense of stillness, as if all the tension from the session had dissipated into the night. Ryland now understood the layer of paradise offered to the couples seeking help for their troubles. The scenery stilled her mind and lulled her restless heart.

"So..." Sherrie piped up. "You're welcome to stay the night if you want to give this place a full day of an experience. Then after that we can talk about patient planning." She spoke that last line with such an infliction in her voice, it almost sounded like she was pleading for them to stay.

"That's an idea," Ryland spoke up, although her inquisitive glance floated to Charlie, unsuspecting of his already eyes on her. She couldn't make out the expression on his face, even when standing under the pole lights scattered across the ranch.

But his response was bewildering. "Sure," Charlie asserted with a gentle nod.

Appraisal lifted the looks of the Turners as Maxwell exclaimed, "Excellent!" Then his left shoulder leaned back as he lifted an arm and pointed in the direction behind him. "If you keep heading that way, you'll find the Common Hall, where you can eat or relax. We'll send our daughter to take you to your room in a bit."

The couple thanked the Turners before heading to the Common Hall, which took about five minutes. As they neared the Hall, they had more source of light with the help of more light poles and a well-lit bonfire as a centerpiece of what looked like the outdoor lounge. There were cushioned benches and lounge chairs strategically placed in symmetrical order. The eerie cloak that smothered the atmosphere of the ranch was abruptly lifted by increasingly audible sounds of laughter and the lighthearted patter of voices. As soon as Charlie pushed against one of the paired heavy oak doors, the liveliness on the other side bombarded the couple all at once like a gust of wind.

The place was vast in space and buzzed with activity. Ryland's eyes followed the train of options that unfolded before them. It was a beautiful mod-arcadian environment with wooden beams lining the ceiling, which acted as a solid foundation for the high-hung lanterns. The people were seated in elongated benches organized around the room in a five-by-five setup. On Ryland's right was a fireplace kindled with animated flames. There was enough space between the right column of benches and the fireplace itself for a few cliques of people to huddle around it. As for the wall on the other side of the room, it was mostly made of floor-to-ceiling windows. At the far back of the room, an idyllic kitchen with a brick oven churned out the smell of something freshly baked like warm bread or roasted herbs. Ryland was glad the noise of the heavily packed hall concealed her demanding stomach.

At first, the couple was hesitant on where to start. After watching a group head to a window counter that separated the kitchen from the main area, they decided food was a more favorable option. Charlie took the lead in that direction. As the pair made their way to the kitchen, someone sprouted from one of the benches and leapt in their path. Charlie almost told the person off until he and Ryland immediately recognized the chopped midnight hair swaying around her petite round face and those piercing eyes, which were always studying and often contrasted her glossy girlish smile.

Instead of her usual strange outfits, she was dressed like everyone on the ranch, except for the same tiny denim shorts Ryland recalled from the dinner. She had a lollipop in her hand and a dazzle in her eyes at the sight of the couple. "Sabrina?" Ryland called out.

"Yep!" she answered. Then she wrapped her arms around them. "I'm so glad you came!"

Ryland had grown used to Sabrina by this point, so she returned the embrace. It seemed that Charlie had already become comfortable with Sabrina because his mood lit up enough to brighten the room. "Boy, is it nice to see a familiar face!"

Sabrina waved him off, playfully. "Aw! You'll get used to things around here," she assured. Before either of the pair could respond, Sabrina quickly added, "Come sit with me!" Then she folded back into her spot on the benches without checking if Ryland and Charlie would follow suit.

As the couple wedged themselves beside Sabrina, she remarked, "I heard about your first session today. How'd you like it?" As she spoke, Sabrina picked up her fork and started poking at her bowl-filled pasta.

Charlie went on to explain, "It's something we'll never forget. Lots of stories that are still playing in my head." Ryland's brows raised at Charlie. She almost voiced her bewilderment but thankfully Sabrina stopped her.

"Yeah, my parents are gnarly when it comes to couples' therapy," she described.

Parents? Ryland's mind echoed. Giving herself a wide view of Sabrina, her eyes scanned the young Turner. Ryland marveled at how she missed the strong resemblance between Sabrina and Sherrie.

"I remember once I sat in a session and this one lady bawled her eyes out. Her baseline is pretty much *mysterious.* Her husband, on the other hand... *Oof!* He's like a *junkyard dog*! He wasn't in the session, at the time, but they had a huge fight prior. My parents practically swooped in and revived what was left of her confidence."

Ryland's heart sank. Hearing that story sent her back to when her father was still around. Estranged by day, disturbed by night. That's exactly how he treated Mama and Callie. Suddenly, his rage manifested in her ears. He felt so present that Ryland neatly jumped in her own skin. But as quick as it came, the reminder was snuffed out like a flame when Charlie's hand rested on her knee. He gave it a gentle squeeze, as if saying, "I'm right here."

"But enough of that," Sabrina commented. "I really hate those kinds of topics. Let's find somewhere peaceful so we can chit chat before I take you to your room."

Ryland nearly thanked her and judging by Charlie's face, he seemed grateful for the relief. The threesome slipped out of the benches and beelined for the door. Sabrina was satisfied with the outdoor lounge, although it was occupied by a few cliques. Some were eating, others played cards. Among the crowd, a guy sat crisscrossed on one of the tables with a caramel brown guitar perched in his lap. His fingers strummed against the bronze strings as they sparkled an enthralling tune. His blonde hair captured a glow in the moonlight as it appeared tousled so effortlessly over his enigmatic eyes, which were a careful blend of golden and emerald hues. He whistled a tune that danced with the softness of the air, and he was encamped by a group of faces that beamed in the firelight as they gazed up at him. Even Ryland admitted to the beautiful notes that serenaded her ears. Her stare shifted to Charlie as she was reminded of those tough nights when she was rocked back to sleep by his beautiful voice.

Sabrina whistled in awe, stirring the blond to peer up through his lashes in her direction. His lips were tugged into a sheepish grin before his eyes flew back down to his hands. Ryland immediately noticed the smile lingering on Sabrina's face, but it was just a glimpse before the young Turner ducked her countenance behind her raven hair. Instead of questioning it, Ryland let herself be led to an isolated table, which sat a few feet away from the rest of the crowd. As soon as the trio got comfortable in their spots, Sabrina leaned forward with her elbows resting in her knees and her chin planted in her palm. She trained her focus on the couple and proceeded to ask about their origins. Like where they came from? How did Charlie and Ryland meet? How long have they been together? Why did they want to get married? Finally, Sabrina popped the question, "Why a pre-honeymoon?"

Ryland, who was sandwiched between Charlie on her right and Sabrina on her left, answered, "Our lives have been saturated with wedding planning lately. We thought it would be great to pull away from everyone and just enjoy each other."

"*Aw*, I wanted to ask about the planning," Sabrina replied. "I understand it's stressful."

"In a way, no," Charlie piped up. "But also, yes in a few ways. It's mostly the invite list."

Sabrina responded with an arch of her brow at him. "Oh, too many to sort out?"

"More like trying to figure out if some people on the list are worth the headache," Ryland spilled. She didn't mean to. Her mouth was quicker than her mind. She tried to redact the somberness of what was said by adding, "But we'll figure it out eventually."

Sabrina leaned back as her gaze drifted to the blonde in the center of the courtyard. "I understand that part," she said, half to herself.

Ryland almost asked what she meant by that, but Sabrina quickly bounced back. She perked up with the same sweet grin Ryland came to know. With a honeyed tone, the young Turner asked, "Are you two ready to settle for the night? I don't want to keep you up. Trust me, I'll talk your ear off!"

Ryland chuckled in response. "Sure," she said. "I think I could definitely use a hot shower and some sleep." Usually, the fiery belle would be on the hunt for a meal by now, but her nerves stole any ounce of hunger. Still, Ryland looked to Charlie, who was unsurprisingly on the same page.

Thankfully for the couple, Sabrina respected their wishes. As she stood up to lead them to where they can rest their heads, Ryland spotted the lingering gaze in Sabrina's eyes as the trio bypassed the blond to start the path to their destination.

As they inched farther from the warmth of the bonfire and the pole lights, the darkness thickened around them. Sabrina fished a flashlight from her pocket and aimed its blazing beam ahead of them. Goosebumps laced Ryland's exposed skin as she became hyper aware of their surroundings. As they passed over a particular path, Charlie asked Sabrina if he could retrieve their stuff from the car. That was a twenty-minute task, not including getting back to the direction of their place. Just as Ryland's legs felt as if they might give way, they approached a cabin with a beautiful lawn of lush grass and cactus with flower buds growing out of them. Although in the streak of light coming from Sabrina's flashlight, the facade was like Wonderland after midnight. The cabin itself was simple with the same bucolic allure as all the other buildings on the ranch. A faint scent of spicy wood and pine complimented the night air surrounding the cabin.

"This is it!" Sabrina announced. How she spoke with as much energy as the start of their hike was beyond Ryland, who was out of breath despite her own athleticism.

Charlie seemed to have recovered a bit quicker than Ryland. She was thankful she didn't have to speak as Charlie replied to Sabrina, "Thanks a million! Anything we should know about this place?"

Sabrina nodded. "Flashlights are on your nightstands," she started down the list of things to be aware of. "I wouldn't recommend staying out too late on the porch unless tussling with coyotes is your thing. There is an emergency kit on the wall, along with the fire extinguisher. All you have to do is smash the glass. Your only weapon is the hatchet. Otherwise, this place is totally comfortable with electricity and, yes, hot, clean water!"

Ryland was sold by that last part. Her muscles really needed it after all that walking. The trio bid each other goodnight after the couple thanked Sabrina again. As Charlie stepped toward the door, it dawned on Ryland that they forgot to ask for a key until a sharp click yanked her attention in Charlie's direction. "How did you...?" slipped out of her mouth.

Charlie waved a shiny card-shaped object in her view. "She gave it to me while I was grabbing our stuff from the car."

"Huh..." Ryland let out, but then chose to be silent. Instead, she followed Charlie into their place until she nearly bumped into his back. She almost called him out for it until her eyes swept the room.

"*Woah!*" they chorused.

The interior was sharp and elegant, contrasting the humble cottage appeal outside. It was a one-bedroom spot with a lovely parlor room. The medium-sized loveseat was an emerald green and the curtains had a shade that was a mix of blush pink, and beige. The floorboards showcased a mahoney color with a glossed finish. The wall decor was a blend of romantic bronze-framed paintings and bohemian knick-knacks, which strangely complimented the cabin's rich caramel walls. Their bedroom was just as breathtaking with a queen-sized bed that stood out like a sore thumb and soft airy curtains that resembled linen. On the bed was a fluffy cream duvet set and fun-shaped pillows. Spread out neatly underneath the bed was a large round rug the same shade as their couch. On either side were matching deep brown nightstands and cream-colored table lamps. Perched neatly next to the lamps were individual flashlights, just as Sabrina promised. The couple also found the emergency kit and the hatchet in their designated places.

"I'm thoroughly confused," Charlie let out. "I know it's a resort but... wow!"

Ryland simply shrugged, more drawn to the bed. She almost sank as she flopped backwards with arms stretched out, like she might make a snow angel in the sheets. "Hey, they have to revive relationships somehow," she commented. "I'd probably make the stay-ins like this too."

"I don't know..." Charlie murmured as he walked about their cabin. Eventually, he circled back to the bedroom and sat on the edge where Ryland was. As he peered down at her, Ryland immediately caught the wheels in his troubled dark pools. She lifted herself by the elbows until she was at eye-level with him. "Do you really want to stay here?" he asked her, his voice laced with earnestness.

The scarlet rose jonesed for him to say yes, but she had to be fair. "Let's see how this plays out tomorrow," she pitched. "If this place is what I believe it is, let's give it two weeks. That's all I think we need."

Charlie's beautiful features contorted into a wince. His bottom lip was once again between his teeth, something Ryland learned that he always did when he was at a crossroad. The moment of his silence seemed to drag on with tension hanging over them, until finally, he caved in. "Okay," he agreed. "Two weeks." Relief and excitement washed over Ryland. Her arms flew around him as she pecked his temple. He responded with a gentle squeeze of her shoulder as he rested his cheek on top of her head. "Let's get some sleep..." he suggested.

That Ryland had no protest.

CHAPTER NINE

That night, Ryland found herself in a different place—but it was not unfamiliar. The four walls around her were adorned with crayon drawings and oversized cartoon character stickers, their bright colors almost overwhelming. Shelves leaned against those walls, crammed with plush toys, books, and whimsical knick-knacks, the sort of trinkets that reflected the boundless imagination of childhood. She sat on the edge of a twin bed, wrapped in frilly blankets and pillows, a swirl of cotton-pink, cream, and metallic sparkles that made her feel as though she were at the omphalos of a dream.

Ryland's gaze shifted to the mirror of her childhood vanity, standing directly across from her. Reflected back were her familiar ginger ringlets, slicked back into a near-neat ponytail by a soft blue bow, while the rest cascaded down her back like a fiery cloud. Gone were the white tube top and dark gray leggings she had fallen asleep in. Instead, she wore a satin checkered dress of white and blue, its boat neck bodice flowing into a flared skirt. Pearl studs glittered on her ears, matching the bracelet that adorned her wrist. Her eyes did not neglect the pink softcover Bible held protectively in her arms.

Her fingers lifted instinctively, tracing the familiar freckles scattered across her face. But she caught the glint of sadness in her brown eyes—and she knew why. Slowly, dread seeped into her, creeping up her spine as her ears picked up the unmistakable sound of heavy footsteps passing her door. And then came her mother's voice, bellowing through the house.

Ryland clutched the only hope in her arms tighter to her chest, feeling as though her ribs might collapse under the weight of the memory. She knew this day. Her mother's scolding words, "*You* are the reason we are always late!" still made her flinch. But worse was the laugh that followed. Cold and hostile, it reverberated around the house, sending chills through her skin. "It's

2006, and idiots still follow religion!" he had taunted. A bottle shattered against a wall, and Ryland couldn't tell what was louder—the breaking glass or the deafening thud of her heart in her ears.

Ryland nearly jumped out of her skin as her door creaked open, her breath catching in her throat like a trapped bubble. Her arms trembled, clutching the Bible tighter still, though she dared not let them fall. But then—just as abruptly—Callie's face appeared. Even at thirteen, Callie was radiant. She had sleek, midnight-black hair styled in a half-up, half-down fashion, with a perfect French bang that framed her deep brown eyes lined with lashes thick enough to appear drawn on. She wore a cornsilk-yellow sundress with puffed sleeves that hemmed just above her elbows. Her favorite heart-shaped locket rested just above the neckline, gleaming a bright gold in the light. And, of course, she had a matching yellow bow in her hair. Ryland had always thought yellow was Callie's color. Whenever her sister wore it, she'd call her "Belle," and in her eyes, no one was more deserving of the name.

Ryland leaped from her bed, calling out to her sister, and ran into her arms. But just as quickly as solace came, the room of pastels was devoured by reality, yanking her back to where she was lying down beside Charlie's sleeping face. His dark lashes brushed lightly against his cheeks, and his breathing was even. Dazed and overwhelmed in the moment, all Ryland could do was observe him from afar. As her eyes drank him in, warmth bubbled up daintily from behind the walls of her chest. Reflexively, her hand reached out with fingers brushing through the softness of his hair. Then she lingered there, and just stared at him.

But something inside her shifted, as whatever budded within collapsed on itself. She withdrew her hand and shook her head, as though snapping out of a trance, and slid out of bed as quietly as she could. The distance between them seemed to grow as she left the room, but remnants of his touch were like tingles on her hand.

She wandered to the small loveseat in their cabin's living space. The coolness of the fabric greeted her, but her thoughts were still swirling. There was more brewing within her than she realized and it had taken root long before the couple arrived at the ranch. She lifted her phone to her face, though she didn't remember picking it up along the way to the couch, and her fingers dialed a number she knew by heart.

After a few rings, a familiar voice crackled through the speaker.

"Hello?"

"Belle..." Ryland's voice came out frail but weighted.

"Rye!" Callie's excitement on the other end was immediate. "What are you doing up? It's almost three in the morning!"

Ryland laughed softly, shaking her head. "Yeah, I know. Sleep just isn't on the agenda tonight, I guess."

"Sis, you *have* to stop worrying about the wedding. I know it's a lot, but everything's fine."

Ryland's smile lifted her face. Callie always knew how to comfort her, even from a distance.

"Trust me, I know," Ryland assured, though she couldn't hide the doleful tone leashed around her voice. "It's not the wedding that's keeping me up."

A faint shuffling sound came from the other end of the line. Ryland could picture Callie settling into her usual spot—propping herself up with pillows like she often did when she sensed something in their conversations.

"What's going on?" Callie finally asked, her timbre more alert but gentle.

Ryland hesitated for a moment. "Charlie and I... we're at this place for couples. It's nice here, honestly. Peaceful—somewhere I'd think about staying for a few days, at least."

"Yet, you don't like this 'couples' place," Callie inserted with a knowing lilt to her tone.

Ryland let out a sigh, running a hand through her already-tousled hair. "It's not that I don't like it. I do. There's something almost... grounding about it." Then, she paused as her eyes drifted to the bedroom. "But Charlie doesn't feel the same way. There's been this strange shift between us ever since we came here. I can sense it..."

"You think he's getting cold feet?"

"No, I don't think it's that," Ryland replied, shaking her head as if trying to convince herself. "It seems like... he's not into the idea of allowing someone to help us. He's always been so *self-reliant*, you know? But here, with everyone offering advice, support... it's like he's closed off."

"Help?" Callie repeated, sharply, her voice laced with concern. "Are you two in trouble? Ryland, what's going on?"

Ryland swallowed hard, her eyes squeezing shut as she forced the words out. "It's a retreat... for couples who want therapy." The confession felt more like a stone in her throat.

Callie scoffed so incredulously. "You and Charlie? Therapy? Now? You're getting married in six weeks, Ryland!"

"I know!" Ryland defended, almost too quickly. She felt her words fall to the pit of her stomach. "But how am I supposed to get married when I feel haunted *all the time*? I can't just ignore what's going on inside me."

Callie's voice flattened, which only added to Ryland's guilt. "So, you're the one with cold feet, then."

The thought alone felt like a sharp blow. "No!" she fired back. "I *love* Charlie. I can't imagine being with anyone else. It's just... I need help, Callie. I need someone to help me figure all this out, and I can't do it on my own."

"Do what on your own?" Callie pressed, but Ryland got choked up in silence, her face dropping to her hand. Finally, her sister's discernment kicked in. "I see where this is going."

On the other end of the line, Ryland heard a bit of shuffling and the soft patter of feet. Then, a familiar, deep and resonant voice called out faintly in the background. It was Callie's husband, David, probably stirring in his sleep at the sound of her on the phone.

"It's okay, babe," Callie called back softly. "If Nathanael wakes up, all he needs is his bottle. There's tea in it—just heat it up and give it to him."

Ryland's heart plumed at the mention of her nephew. Nathanael was only 15 months old, but his existence brought so much joy to Callie's life. The scarlet rose wondered how that would be for her and Charlie. Then, there was a beat of silence between the sisters, followed by the sound of a sliding door shutting. Ryland could imagine Callie now standing on the balcony of their home, taking a deep breath before speaking again.

"Listen to me good," Callie insisted, her voice swelling with conviction. "You're not her, Ryland. You'll never be like Mama. Look at me and David—we've been married seven years, and trust me, it wasn't always easy. But we made it through. So will you and Charlie. You just have to leave it in God's hands."

"I have to do my part, too," Ryland countered, her words tinged with frustration. She knew how to pray, but lately, her prayers had felt more like whispers lost in the wind.

"Of course," Callie agreed gently. "But you're not meant to carry everything on your own. There are some things you have to let go of, Ryland. You can't control it all. Please believe that much."

Ryland's eyes closed, a heavy sigh slipping through her lips. She had been told this before, but the weight was too enormous, too complex.

"Okay..." she relented. "I hear you."

"Good," Callie said, triumphantly. "I love you so much. If you start to feel like this again, don't hesitate to call me. Promise?"

"Sure..."

Then the sisters exchanged goodbyes. But before Ryland could hang up, she heard the faint cry of Nathanael from the other end of the line. His tiny whimpers pierced the stillness of the night. And just like that, the ache returned with a vengeance that same haunting feeling as before. The darkness of the past loomed in the corners of her mind, threatening to swallow her whole.

Ryland spent the remaining hours on the couch. Her thoughts would thread more memories only for them to become loose and out of reach, before taunting her again. Ryland fought until the faint light of dawn spilled over the horizon. But on the outside, she was limp like a corpse, except her eyes which slowly blinked at the realization that she never did go back to sleep. She tilted her head back until she found a digital clock on the coffee table across from the couch. It was 6 a.m.. With a grieved sigh, she pulled herself to her feet, and went about her morning routine.

After a quick, refreshing shower, she slipped into a pair of jeans—practical and ready for the morning air. She accommodated them with a faded Blink-182 tee, an old gift from Callie after she came back from their concert in 2010, worn out by time. Ryland gathered her thick red curls, braiding them back so no strand would obscure her vision. She loved the wildness of her hair but often wondered what it would be like to cut it shorter, maybe even to a bob.

Before heading out, Ryland paused for a moment, lingering in the threshold with her hand resting on the doorknob. Her stare traveled toward the room where Charlie still slept, his figure like still art beneath the creme-colored covers. She lingered only a second longer, then agilely closed the door behind her. Stepping into the morning, her lungs drank in the warm air, which felt like a balm pouring down her throat. But as quickly as serenity came, it was taken over by an alarming thought. She had no plan, not even a destination. All she knew was the vague direction of the Common Hall, but beyond that, the world was nothing else but open and aimless.

"I need a map," she muttered to herself. With that, a goal slowly took shape, however small it was.

As Ryland walked further, she observed how the cabins were nestled in a thoughtful layout, creating a cozy, tucked-away feel. Each one had an outer appearance that was Arcadian and whimsical in its glory, the kind of idyllic beauty that made Ryland feel like she was in the middle of a folktale. The cabins were situated in a makeshift cul-de-sac, with her and Charlie's cabin at the tail end, secured behind lush green shadows. The pathway she walked curved around the housing area in a gentle loop, allowing each cabin to feel secluded yet connected. The open spaces between the cabins were dotted with patches of Arizona wildflowers, with lanterns hanging on wooden posts at intervals along the walkways.

"I didn't notice any of this last night," Ryland mused. She imagined how easy it would be to get lost among these winding trails, how the allure of it all could make a person feel like they were in a different world.

The further she walked, the more cabins disappeared out of plain view. Eventually, the scarlet rose found herself standing in larger land. Up ahead from where she stood was a stretch of fenced-in pasture. She then followed the wooden gates until a stable appeared in her sights. She quickened her pace with the hope of running into someone who could give her direction.

As she neared the entrance, Ryland heard the familiar but soothing snorts of horses, along with murmuring voices. The stable was fairly intimidating in stature, as Ryland counted all ten stalls. In each stall stood a horse with a different coat: most had classic brunette brown, two were a pale gray shade, one sported a reddish chestnut hue, and the last, striking among the rest, had a glossy black coat. Tending to these breathtaking creatures were two women, gently feeding them alfalfa hay. Their movements were delicate, and yet efficient, displaying a calm familiarity with the horses.

Immediately, Ryland recognized one of the women. The same woman looked up with piercing, familiar eyes that locked onto Ryland. This woman was no longer in the flowy summer dress from the day before, but instead sported a flannel and skinny jeans with a stylish pair of flats. Her raven tresses spilled around her shoulders yet cuffed behind her ears, exposing a beautiful set of diamond studs. Her cheeks were painted with a peach hue and her face lifted into an illuminating grin as she waved her over.

Ryland reflected her smile and called out a soft, "Morning!"

When she was much closer to the Turner, Sherrie, already feeding one of the gray horses, greeted her. "It's nice to see you again!" Then she paused to stroke the horse's neck before turning her attention back to Ryland. "How was your first night?"

Ryland shrugged slightly. "It usually takes a while before I get used to a new environment."

Sherrie arched a brow. "So you're considering staying?"

Ryland simply shrugged. "I think it'd be good."

"And your fiancé?" Sherrie inquired, though her smile tainted a bit. Ryland brushed it off as mere eagerness, but the image lingered.

"He's getting there," she replied, but even in her ears, her words were fragile. "I think he might need another session."

Sherrie's smirk deepened, her eyes twinkling with understanding. "Well, now he has a full day," she pitched amusingly.

Ryland gave the thought a silent nod. But she quickly changed the subject. Her eyes scanned each stall, drawn to the quiet, powerful beauty of the horses. "Are they open to everyone?" she asked, curiosity piqued.

"For therapy, under heavy supervision, yes," Sherrie said, flatly. "Not for free riding. It's nothing personal. Just... not everyone can handle a horse. Then, there are lawsuits. They are practically the death of an independent business like ours if there's an injury on-site."

Ryland bobbed along. "I wouldn't risk it either."

Sherrie continued tending to the horses as she added, "Speaking of therapy,... the daily structure is four sessions a day. We have our main group in the morning after breakfast, which ends at ten, then workshops start at twelve pm. Lunch is between one and three pm. At five, we regroup as a whole."

Ryland perked up at the sound of a full schedule, but she was still left in wonder. "Is there a way to get around the ranch? I've been looking for a map."

Sherrie's eyes widened with concern as her mouth formed a soft "O." "You poor thing!" she exclaimed. "You must've been wandering all over this place. It's a fairly safe area, but we still have to watch out for wildlife."

Ryland chuckled as Sherrie picked up the pace with feeding the horses. Once sure of their satisfaction, Sherrie moved towards a satchel resting on the ground near one of the stalls. From it, she fished out a piece of paper folded in four. A glint of recognition sparkled in her eyes as she took her place beside Ryland with the paper unfolded, explaining the layout of the ranch. As Sherrie pointed out various buildings, pathways, and specific landmarks, Ryland absorbed every detail, her mind locking onto each word—a trait she had possessed since childhood.

Sherrie's kindness extended further when she handed the map to Ryland, who accepted it gratefully, knowing Charlie would need it as well.

After expressing her thanks, Ryland set off again, this time with a refreshed sense of direction.

CHAPTER TEN

Ryland mulled over the options as she tried to pinpoint something that grabbed her attention. Hiking? Landscape photography? Maybe breakfast first. There wasn't much else to do at the moment since the other activities she was interested in didn't start until 8 am. Ryland peered down at her wristwatch, which read: 7:00 AM. She huffed at the thought of having too much time and too little to do. Then—in the middle of raking through her thoughts—her mind traveled back to Charlie, who she hoped was awake by now.

So she trekked back to their cabin.

This second round of walking there seemed easier than last night. By the time she made it up the two-step porch to their front door, Ryland wasn't as winded. As she slipped back inside, she called out to her fiancé. But only silence lingered in the air.

Ryland scanned the parlor room for his familiar face, but there was no trace of him. She checked the bedroom but, again, didn't find him. "Maybe he's in the bathroom?" she said to herself. But, of course, he wasn't there. The door was open and the lights were off. *Where is he?* she wondered. Her mind started to reach for the panic switch when a set of footsteps drew close behind her. She whipped around—with her heart in her ears—quickly registering that she had left the front door still agape. She half-expected an animal to have wandered inside, but instead, she was met with adrenalized sienna eyes. Before she could voice her fears, Charlie's arms eased her into his embrace.

"You scared me for a second, dove," he said, his voice tender in her ear.

"I just needed a walk," Ryland replied. She pulled back just enough to peer up at him, considering that he was nearly a foot taller than her. "I didn't get much sleep, and I didn't want to wake you. I figured I could use the time to clear my head."

Charlie's hand was delicate on her cheek, his skin caressing hers, as he assured, "I wouldn't have minded if you woke me up. I'm still here for you. You know that, right?"

Ryland simply nodded and leaned into his palm but chose to lock away what she wanted to tell him. Instead, she let him in about her encounter with Sherrie and handed him the map. As he examined its marks, she asked, "What do you think we should do since the first session doesn't start till ten?" She looked at her watch again. It was now thirty minutes past the hour.

Charlie folded the map and said, "There's a lake behind us. Remember how we used to hang out at Ashurst?" He slipped it inside the pocket of his dark jeans, which he paired with a Def Leppard tee-shirt tucked into his pants, revealing his favorite black belt with a statement silver buckle. Half to himself, he added, "I'm starving, though. Now I know why it's a bad idea to skip dinner."

Ryland's attention drifted to his hair, and she marveled at how quickly it had returned to its natural curls. She loved it that way. Her hand moved on its own, fingers threading through his long, dark chestnut strands. Her eyes traveled to his face—allowing herself to relish his beauty—until it dawned on her that his mouth was still moving.

"Ryland?"

"Huh?"

She tried shaking herself back to the present moment, as only a part of her returned. But most of Ryland remained lost. Still, she forged a grin, hoping it was enough to appease him. "I'm alright... just *tired*."

His eyes narrowed as he searched her face. Then after what felt like forever, he turned away and headed for the door. "We should make it in time for breakfast," was all he said.

And just like that, he left his scarlet rose standing there, baffled and dejected.

The couple spent the morning in silence toward one another but made some acquaintances while dining in the Common Hall. Ryland clicked with two in particular—Cheyenne, from their very first session, and another woman around Ryland's and Cheyenne's age, named Tithia. Cheyenne stayed true to the bubbly nature Ryland was introduced to, while Tithia seemed elegant with her words and graceful in the way she moved.

Whenever she spoke, Ryland caught a flicker of wisdom in her steady russet-brown eyes, which were striking against her honey complexion. Her sleek ponytail, dyed a dark but shiny blonde hue, danced behind her like a gold tassel.

The trio clicked instantly, which brightened Ryland's mood in a way she hadn't realized she needed. Although, she was often pulled away whenever she heard Charlie's laugh or felt his arm brush against hers. At one point, Charlie leaned against Ryland while talking to the people he had aligned with, including the blond guitarist from last night. She couldn't resist the awareness of him, despite her failed attempts to will her mind. A part of her wondered if Charlie felt the same way.

Ryland seemed to have found a part of that question answered when Charlie slipped his hand in hers as they walked to the cottage house where their last group session was held. As they walked, Ryland noticed Tithia parting ways from the crimson-haired darling and Cheyenne. Tithia and Cheyenne quickly explained that there were three groups. Ryland, Charlie, and Cheyenne were in the third group. Charlie's new acquaintances were in the second one.

The young couple followed suit by joining their group in a circle in the middle of the room. Ryland appreciated the sunlight streaming through the windows, washing away the uncanny vibes from last time. Cheyenne, along with Xavier, sat beside Ryland and Charlie, with the women in the middle of the foursome, adding to Ryland's ease. Yet, as the group waited expectantly for a counselor to walk in, the atmosphere was still. No one spoke, which triggered a new wave of bewilderment within the crimson-haired darling. She looked to Charlie, but once again, his attention was elsewhere. Resting his chin in the cup of his hand, he was long lost in thought.

Ryland opened her mouth to whisper to Charlie, but a soft hand rested on her other arm. As she turned to face the person who wanted her attention, Cheyenne lifted a finger to her lips. *Odd*, Ryland thought, but she reasoned that maybe this moment was meant for reflection before going into counseling.

After what felt like an eternity, Sherrie and Maxwell popped their heads into the room. Everyone looked their way, including Ryland, but Charlie remained distracted. "Good morning, everyone!" Sherrie cheered, now in her usual knee-length, flowy dress—this one a pastel green that strangely harmonized with her striking emerald eyes. Her raven-colored tresses were pulled back in a high ponytail, and wrapped around her head was a dark green silk headband. Maxwell wore a matching shirt, tucked into a brighter pair of denim jeans. His graying sandy hair was combed back, revealing his smiling blue eyes.

"It's nice to see our visitors are here with us a second time," he commented, staring directly at Charlie and Ryland. "I hope you're able to stay for the day."

Ryland flashed a polite grin, while Charlie remained unmoved by the sound of the Turners in the room. However, his attention *was* on them. Ryland marveled at the way his eyes turned on like radars, scanning every movement around him.

The Turners found their places in the same spot as before. As soon as they settled in, the session began.

"With it being Friday," said Maxwell, "I'd like for us to talk about what we are grateful for about our partners." Someone in the circle started to raise their hand, but Maxwell's head swiftly turned toward the young couple, narrowing his focus on Charlie. "How about you two? It's okay to join the conversation, if you'd like." Though, it didn't sound like much of an option.

Ryland noticed a particular fixation on Charlie, and she couldn't fathom why. Then again, maybe Maxwell could pick up on things faster than most, given his expertise.

Ryland saw a glimmer of hope when Charlie decided to take on the challenge. In that moment, she found herself engulfed in his loving gaze. As he spoke, her hand remembered his, as both hands remained interlocked. "I appreciate the way you know me more than anyone," he confessed aloud. He didn't go any further, but it was enough for her. She tried her might to fight back the smile forming on her face, but it was a losing battle. So, she dropped her gaze, hoping to hide the warm hue on her cheeks.

Maxwell, however, did not appear satisfied. "Do you think you could explore that a bit?" he coaxed. "Kind words are always soothing, but many times we don't realize our partners are looking for something specific from us to recognize in them."

His words knocked down Ryland's smile, bringing back the noise in her mind from earlier. But Charlie spoke up again. "We've been together for six years," he explained. "In these later years, I feel like we've become more grounded." Glancing at Ryland, he added, "At least, I think so."

That felt both relieving and crushing. At one point, she believed they *were* more grounded than ever. But lately, she'd been questioning if she truly trusted that. Nonetheless, Charlie's response was enough to keep Maxwell at bay. Ryland almost thought she saw Maxwell's jaw clench. But in a flash, his face brightened as he turned to other members of the circle.

The session felt as though it lasted for hours when it was actually about thirty minutes long. As everyone scattered to places they had planned for the day, the Turners beelined toward the scarlet rose and her fiancé.

"Hey, you two!" Sherrie greeted, winking at Ryland. "So... what's the word?"

Charlie rested his eyes on Ryland. It was evident that he was willing to go at her pace. But she was more grateful for the consoling grin on his face as he coaxed her with a nod. That was another thing she loved about him—he was a man of his word. To the Turners, she affirmed, "We're in."

Sherrie's face pulled back as a cheer escaped her, practically bouncing beside Maxwell. "I'm so stoked for you to be a part of us! You two have so much potential here."

Maxwell rested his hand on Charlie's shoulder and gave it a firm shake. "And here I thought you were gonna put up a fight," he bantered. "I guess I can put away the bull ropes now."

Sherrie chuckled along as she and her husband led the young couple up a hill, away from the bustling hub of the ranch, toward what looked like a country home. It was a beautiful shade of ivory that glowed in the sunlight. The house spread about 2,300 square feet and was crowned with a cross-hipped roof. The surroundings were greener than the rest of the ranch, with a white horse being guided within the acres a few yards from where the house stood. Ryland was stunned. She didn't recall seeing this marked on the map.

Maxwell opened the door and allowed Ryland and Charlie to step inside their home. They were led to an office with Maxwell's name plated on the door. The office showcased many of the Turner's achievements and awards. Ryland was especially captivated by a collection of self-authored books on the highest tier of his 4-story bookshelf.

Maxwell maneuvered behind his desk and retrieved two manila folders. He grabbed a nearby Sharpie and wrote down each of their names. Neither Ryland nor Charlie noticed that Sherrie had slipped away until she reappeared with papers tucked under her arm. The fiery darling quickly noted that they were contracts. Butterflies swarmed her insides as she glanced at Charlie, who was already analyzing each printed line.

She, too, studied the paperwork for herself. After a while of internalizing what she needed, Ryland borrowed a pen from Sherrie. As she scribbled her name, Charlie leaned into her ear. "Are you sure you want to do this?"

Ryland peered up at him, his question clouding her mind with confusion. "It's only for two weeks, remember?" she reminded him.

Charlie didn't respond right away. Instead, he glanced back down at the papers in his hands. Ryland held her breath as she watched the tug-a-war behind his eyes until, finally, he let out a sigh and reached for the same pen as well. Once both signatures were documented, Sherrie collected the papers. Her grin widened as she said, "You two should be proud of yourselves. This is quite a step. Trust me, you won't regret it."

That was what Ryland needed to hear. "What do we do now?" she asked.

Maxwell lifted a hand, aiming toward the door. "You're free to explore the ranch. You will meet with your assigned counselors on Monday. For now, enjoy the festivities. Saturdays tend to be lively. Sundays are quieter."

Ryland turned to Charlie, giving him a reassuring smile. A sense of contentment washed over her, as a part of the scarlet rose returned to a peaceful state. Charlie took her by the hand and led them back outside to the ranch, but not before the couple thanked the Turners.

As they stepped into the warmth of the sun, the two of them permitted themselves a peaceful stroll. Charlie lifted Ryland's hand to his lips, which were soft and warm against her skin. But his eyes never left her as he said, "You should know by now... I'm always here for you."

And he meant that. Though it bothered Ryland that she had to be reminded. Why couldn't she simply believe?

CHAPTER ELEVEN

By nightfall, the young couple were burnt out. They planned to crash in for the evening, but their stomachs protested, drawing the couple's attention to them. Charlie, determined not to skip dinner another night, detoured the pair to the Common Hall. Instead of eating their meals inside, they embraced the serenity of the outdoors. They found a table closer to the open land, granting the couple a balance of solitude and a buzzing community. With her head resting on Charlie's shoulder, her eyes fluttered at the sky as she attempted to count each star. But the vastness of them were too many for her to keep up with. Still, her gaze lingered above as well as the spoonful of rice in her mouth.

Just as she reached for another mouthful, a blur of movement caught her eye. Before she could react, Charlie's body vibrated against hers as his voice sliced through the tranquil night. "Hey, man!" he bellowed.

"I was hoping to run into you again," another voice called back. Ryland straightened up quickly as the figure drew closer. Once it was finally under the flickering light of the fire and nearby pole lamps, realization settled in. It was the blond guitarist. As he approached the couple, the fiery darling was taken back at his striking looks now that she had a better view of him. She understood why Sabrina had eyes on him. She even appreciated his flare against the monotonous ranch apparel. His hazel orbs floated to Ryland, which sparkled with recognition. "So, this is who you've been telling me about!"

Her glossed lips lifted into a sheepish grin as she turned back to Charlie, who slipped his arm around her. "She's the one!" he said with such contentment that his words kindled something inside her. Not even the caressing warmth of the bonfire could measure up.

Turning to his new friend, she gave him a soft wave. "Hi, I'm Ryland."

Desmond tilted his head with a new twinkle in his eyes, as he glanced between the couple. "Well that's something," he commented.

Ryland shook her head, mystified by his reaction. Her smile remained unwavering but took on a hint of curiosity. "What do you mean?"

"The land where rye is abundant—that's what your name means," Desmond started to explain. As he spoke, he plotted himself on a boulder neighboring Charlie and Ryland's table. "Rye is one of the most nutritious grains out there, and it can feed many homes." Eyeing Charlie, he added, "We were just talking about the meaning of names the other day. I mentioned how *Charles* means strength or nobility. This was after he told me the meaning of his last name, since I've always been interested in Native American studies."

Ryland perked up, recalling a past night when they were still in school. It was that night she and Charlie deepened their connection as they learned about each other's family roots. Mama's side came from the Hopi tribe, but unlike Ryland, Callie resembled that background more. Ryland looked more like her father. But Charlie pointed out something she never forgot—he still saw her mother's roots in her. It surprised her since Mama always made her feel like the odd one out. That's when she learned of Charlie's family tribes, the Tohono O'odham and the Lakota peoples.

"Yeah, Angpetu means *sun* in the Lakota language," she recited to Desmond.

He nodded, affirmatively. Then, he pointed his attention at her. "What about you?"

"Kootálá," she answered without hesitation. "It usually means glow or light from an ember. I guess it depends who you talk to."

Ryland caught a pleased look in Charlie's eyes on her, while Desmond leaned back, his mind spinning. "So..." the blond started to say, "your family is from the Hopi people...?"

Ryland responded with a certain shake of her head that meant yes and no, but she clarified that, "That's true for my mom. Actually, when she was still married to my father, she held onto her maiden name. She loves her family culture, despite being raised by a Protestant woman. My father's family migrated from Iceland back in the 1940s."

"Iceland? No way!" chirped Desmond. "My parents took us there on a family trip when I was still in middle school. It's such a gorgeous country! What part of Iceland are they from?"

"Kópavogur," said Ryland. "Where'd you visit?"

Desmond leaned forward a bit as the confidence in his grin wavered a bit. "Forgive me if I mispronounce it," he said. "I remember it was *Reykjavík*?"

Ryland let out a laugh. He could use a little help with the accent but, "You said it quite alright," she assured him.

The blond let out a small cheer. Then to the couple he added, jokingly, "You two will have quite the stories to tell your children one day."

"Yeah…" Charlie responded, laughing along. Ryland hoped so. Moreover, she appreciated the twinkle in her fiancé's eyes at the sound of having children someday.

The threesome continued on with small talk and deep thoughts, learning about their backgrounds and the places they've explored. As the conversation went on, Charlie leaned back, seizing an opportunity to trace every angle of her face. Still, there was something indecipherable simmering beneath his affectionate gaze. Ryland tried to sort him out at that moment, but couldn't put her finger on it.

Later that evening, the couple returned to their cabin, hand in hand and heart to heart. Charlie marveled at how much Ryland talked about her father. He rarely heard her speak of him, and when she did, she ended up curled in his arms with tears pouring down his skin. "I'm proud of you, though," Charlie mentioned. "That must've been a big step for you."

Truly, it was.

As the couple neared their door, the scarlet rose spotted something that sent chills through her bones. It was like the earth started to spin under her feet, as her balance threatened to give way. The onyx sky around them felt ten times darker and the darkness heavied like a thickening cloud. Not even the moon above or the flashlights in their hands felt enough. She stopped short in her tracks, hindering Charlie from moving forward. He glanced back at her as concern whelmed in his stare. "What's wrong?" he inquired with worry lines snaking across his forehead.

Ryland couldn't get the words out. So she lifted a finger at what she saw, prompting Charlie to follow her gaze. As soon as his eyes landed on what she saw, all color drained from Charlie's face. "What the heck!" he growled. He marched up the porch steps, despite Ryland's pleas for him not to do so. A sickening taste crawled up her throat. All she could do was watch Charlie yank down a red string taped to their front door, unconcerned of what may be lurking in the shadows that engulfed much of their porch. Then he lifted the string in the air as fury clouded his countenance. "Are we being followed?"

Ryland shook her head. At that point, she wasn't entirely sure. She shifted her head about, looking for any other sign of what they feared. Instead, she found something that rocked her to the core. Some of the other cabins also had red strings taped to their front doors. She swallowed hard then ran to Charlie's side. He looked at her expectantly, but she was too afraid to mention what she saw to him. Instead, she said, "We're surrounded by people, and we still have that map. If anything, we can get some help."

Charlie wasn't entirely convinced but he did not utter a protest. As they stepped inside their place, the dark-haired beau beelined towards the other side of the parlor room, which was a few steps away from their bedroom, and plucked a hatchet from that wall. Though it was merely an attempt to keep the couple safe, the scarlet rose started to wither, pressured by the fear. "Do you think we need that?" she questioned, her voice so small and delicate in her ears.

Charlie walked up to her, though he kept the hatchet hidden behind him. He planted a kiss on her forehead and guided his crimson-haired darling closer to him. "We'll be okay," he said. "I'm just taking extra precautions. That's all."

Ryland conceded with a simple nod. In the back of her mind, she was afraid to sleep that night.

135

CHAPTER TWELVE

Ryland and Charlie didn't enjoy much of the weekend. With very little activities and events, despite what Maxwell promised, it dragged on.

Nonetheless, they were glad to have been alone together. The pair needed time to adjust to their new environment at their own pace. They especially craved rest for their weary minds—but much of their sleep was robbed as neither Charlie nor Ryland could stop staring at the red string he left lying on the parlor room coffee table. When Ryland nudged him to get rid of it, he urged that it was better to keep it. Though he wasn't entirely sure why, or what to do with the string.

Monday came in with a swarm of unanswered questions. But the day still offered a silver lining. The couple finally got used to the flow of a daily schedule, the bit of stability lightly lifting the load on their minds. That only lasted until the end of their morning session.

Sherrie planted herself in the couple's path, blocking their only chance of escape. The crowd diminished in the blink of an eye, soon leaving the scarlet rose and her ebony-haired beau alone with the Turner, whose emerald eyes were trained on Ryland. "I meant to give you the names of your assigned counselors," Sherrie explained, handing Ryland and Charlie their own slip of paper. "I was supposed to slide them in your mailbox before the weekend went out. But I'm glad to have caught you now!" Then she added a detail that even left Ryland baffled. "I changed your schedules personally for the next few days. After group in the mornings, you two have to go to your counselors instead of the workshops."

Charlie arched a brow at her. "Why?"

"It may be because we're new..." Ryland suggested to him.

"Well…" Sherrie counteracted, "that's not entirely the reason. In fact, I only do this with couples I believe need *specific* kinds of help."

"Specific?" Charlie repeated.

Instead of answering his question directly, Sherrie said, "Trust me, it's a compliment. Plus, you're getting married fairly soon, and we only have two weeks. So, I thought we should squeeze in as much work as we can."

With that, Sherrie left the couple alone to tackle a new kind of unknown.

Charlie rested a hand on Ryland's shoulder and said, "Let me take you to your counselor."

But Ryland rejected. "You'll miss yours."

"Don't worry. You come first."

Ryland tussled some more, determined for him to focus on himself, but eventually she caved in. As they walked, the couple realized they were heading back to the cabins, until the road branched out into a different direction. Ryland marveled as the pair discovered a new set of cabins. There weren't as many as the residential side but enough to leave the scarlet rose winded with more questions. Finally, they stopped short in front of one with the numbers 677 plated on the front door. Charlie quickly looked around and back at his own paper, then again at the layout spreading out before him. Even under the brightness of the sun, his eyes clouded.

"What's wrong?" Ryland asked him.

He shook his head, still comparing what he saw to the instructions on his paper. "I guess it'll take me a bit to figure out where mine is..."

"I can walk in on my own," Ryland suggested. "You go ahead and look for yours." That was enough to grab his full attention, though that puzzled look never left his eyes.

"Are you sure?"

Ryland nodded, nudging him to branch out on his own.

But he didn't leave without checking if she still had her phone at the very least. Ryland waved it in the air after quickly fishing it from her jean pocket. Before he had the chance to delay any further, Ryland shooed him away. So he planted a kiss on her cheek and, reluctantly, departed from her.

As soon as she was sure he disappeared down the direction he took, Ryland spun around to face the daunting task awaiting her. She walked up the steps and inhaled deeply, allowing the fresh earthy scent surrounding her to soothe her nerves. After a moment longer of lingering by the door, she mustered the courage to lift her hand, preparing to embrace the hard wood against her knuckles. Her skin barely touched the surface when the door swung open, nearly sending her flying forward.

Now standing in front of Ryland was a woman with wide and bouncy brunette curls, and deep-set blue eyes as mystique as the sea, but warmed at the sight of the startled ginger.

"Hi!" she chirped, beaming a smile at her.

All Ryland could do was wave sheepishly, as her heart was still in her throat. Before she could react any further, Ryland was practically yanked into the cabin. Inside was eccentric compared to the romantic flair of the one she had grown used to. She felt as though she walked into an obsession of the Mad Hatter and his tea party decorum. There were knick knacks of bunnies and fairies, a china cabinet housing a gold and pink teacup set, and the walls were tinted to create a pastel rainbow color scheme. Like many of the makeshift cottages in the hub of the ranch, there was no other room. Just one vast space like a studio apartment. That space was filled with two lilac couches surrounding a round chocolate brown coffee table. Ryland managed to spot a bathroom, which gave her a fleeting hope for a window to escape through. The entire space, despite its folklore appeal, made her feel like Alice—alone and constantly wandering through her mind.

The bouncy brunette took her place on one of the couches and gestured for Ryland to follow suit. At first, she shied away. Then she thought better of it. So, she willed herself to do it. As soon as she was planted on the couch opposite her counselor, the brunette finally introduced herself. "So, I'm Breanna, but you may call me 'Bre' or 'Anna.' I take it you're Ryland, right?"

The scarlet rose nodded.

"Great!" Breanna beamed. "I was hoping it was you. A lot of my clients like to give me surprise visits, but how could I think that when we haven't met? Silly me!"

Ryland tried to forge a smile, but even she didn't feel it in her eyes. It wasn't that she didn't like Breanna—her personality was quite contagious. Instead, Ryland was busy battling the swarm of nerves in her stomach. She wasn't new to the counseling setting. She herself had counseled couples and individuals. But it was hard being on the other end, having to eventually pick at the closet sealing back her skeletons, which threatened to spill out.

Fortunately, Ryland was given a moment to adjust as Breanna described her early achievements, current preferences, and favorite memories. She even talked about her old childhood cat name Monte and how she was thinking of adopting a similar breed soon. Apparently, she really loved Blue Russian cats.

Just when Ryland thought she was free, Breanna brought up the one thing she dreaded. The brunette leaned back on her couch and smiled sweetly, as her chin rested in her hand. "Enough about me," she said. "I want to know more about you…"

Ryland let out a grunt, but dared not let it surface for Breanna's ears to hear. She swallowed hard, sorting out what to say. *Where do I even start?* she asked herself, prying her own mind. After a moment's drag, she opted for something lighthearted. "I'm getting married soon," she offered, but struggled to sound as casual as possible.

Breanna's eyes lit up. "*Ooh!* You must be excited!"

Ryland nodded, letting out a quiet "Yeah…" as her gaze shifted, knowing exactly what she was about to say next. "I'm a bit *worried* too…"

"Worried?" she heard Breanna say. She didn't have to look at her face to see the million unanswered questions written all over it. But the one she asked next held an eerie resemblance to Callie's initial thought. "Are you questioning if he's the one?"

Instead of resorting to the familiar defenses she aimed at her sister, Ryland cowered. She lifted her head and pierced her eyes through Breanna. "I'm questioning if *I'm* the one."

All at once, the brunette's demeanor shifted into something solemn. It was as if she thought Ryland had a different meaning behind her words, but it wasn't. Breanna leaned forward, her expression deepening. "How come you feel that way?"

The troubled darling wanted to say more, but guilt crept into her mind, as echoes of Mama clawed their way back to her. Her voice amplified something startling within Ryland, rocking the walls of her mind. Too disturbed by the noise filling her ears, Ryland quickly shook her head, hoping that was enough to get Breanna to change the subject. Thankfully, her counselor got the signal. Breanna then glanced around the room as Ryland wondered about her motives. Finally, the brunette found what she was looking for. With a grin dancing on her lips, she peered back at Ryland. "Let's have some tea," she pitched. "There's nothing that'll lift your mood like a cup of jasmine with a splash of lemon."

Weirdly, that sparked Ryland back to life. "Really?" she questioned as a chuckle escaped her. Though she was a casual tea drinker, she never experienced the typically hot beverage as something close to therapeutic.

So she gave it a shot.

Ryland left that session with a feeling inside she never had before. She took her first step alone, and it was relieving. She couldn't wait to tell Charlie, except that as soon as she stepped outside, her heart remembered that its other half was not there. She last saw him heading west from where she stood on the porch steps, to find his counselor. It was the same path they took to find her counselor, but she quickly realized it would also guide her back to their cabin. Considering she spent nearly an hour with her counselor, Ryland decided to head for the couple's cabin.

As she neared their place, the same swarm returned with a vengeance and infested her insides with a buzz so loud it reached her ears. Her mind recalled what she admitted to Breanna. *How could I say something like that to Charlie?*

As she stepped inside their cabin, she froze in her tracks. For the first time, she hoped she didn't run into him so soon. Charlie busied himself with a new packet she never saw in his hands before. His back was to her as he rested on the couch with his hair pulled into a bun, allowing her the advantage to see a set of Bluetooth headphones molded into his ears. Slowly, but gradually, she was drawn to the mystery inscribed on those pages. She barely moved an inch from the door when Charlie's eyes flew over his shoulders.

"Oh, when did you get back?" he greeted, unsuspectingly.

She flashed a grin like a kid caught stealing treats from the cookie jar. Then she quickly diverted his attention, nodding at the papers in his hands. "What's that?"

Charlie looked down at his hands, as if he briefly forgot what he was doing moments ago. "Something my counselor wants me to fill out," he explained as Ryland found her place next to him on their couch. She internalized a triumphant cheer as he slid the packet in her hands. "It's pretty much a worksheet, though I didn't expect to do anything like that on my first day with him."

As her eyes carefully traced each line, she too was astonished. But for an entirely different reason. All the prompts and exercises in the packet were best suited for someone struggling with their temper. "Is there something you want to tell me?" she pried, her eyes starting to sting.

Charlie's face twisted as perplexity ate at him. It *was* very pointed of her to ask such a question, but the seconds widened the distance between them. So he put up a fight. "As far as I'm concerned, *no*."

"Really?"

"Really," he said, flatly. "If I need you to know something, I'd tell you."

Ryland narrowed her eyes at him. "No one could ever be *that* open."

Instead of another comeback from Charlie, his head tilted uncannily as he searched her face. She knew what he was looking for, but the scarlet rose refused to rehash her worst nightmare. Still, his lips were pressed tight. Ryland—once convinced to settle the matter just moments ago—collapsed under pressure. Starting to squirm beneath his intense gaze, she finally settled for a truce. Until Charlie beat her to it.

"All you have to do is ask me," he assured her.

Ryland dropped her stare, though his words were already imprinted on her. Instead of saying anything more, she peeled herself off the couch and headed for the bedroom. She kicked herself on the way, wondering how she could jump to such a conclusion. What killed her most is Charlie probably wasn't even aware of the fear that snaked her mind. Inside their room, she slipped out of the baby blue jeans and replaced them with a pair of olive green capri pants. But she kept on the beige t-shirt with a large peace symbol printed on it. Then she traded her cream colored Vans for her favorite hiking shoes. After giving herself a feasible ponytail, she grabbed her phone and earbuds then headed for the door again.

But before her hand touched the knob, his arms wrapped around her. Then his hand reached for hers and eased it from the door. A sigh escaped her but she couldn't tell if it was relief or regret. "I'm sorry..." filled her ears, but it wasn't from her mouth. She spun around and met Charlie's eyes.

"Mind telling me what happened back there between us?" he asked, so invitingly. He lifted a hand to her face then brushed back the stray stands that tickled her lashes.

She shook her head, her eyes ebbing away from him. "I can't..." Before Charlie had the chance to pry, the scarlet rose managed to slip away, like petals flying out of his hands and into the wind.

CHAPTER THIRTEEN

Ryland's feet took on a mind of their own, mechanically leading her away from the cabin. There was no real destination in mind, but the need to escape the walls that seemed to suffocate her and the questions that loomed unanswered. In fact, her mind started to realize that's all she'd been doing lately—running. Charlie's voice, at the moment, wasn't much help either. A part of her knew he didn't do anything wrong. But she was haunted by his tenderness that was too much, too raw. She wasn't ready to face him nor the questions swarming her mind. Not yet.

The air offered some level of solace. As she breathed in, oxygen dripped down her throat like the extract of soothing jasmine leaves. The late afternoon sky was a pale shade of periwinkle, with fading traces of clouds streaking across the limitless dome. It was quite a sight to behold, but Ryland's heart was too heavy for her to notice. She tugged her phone from her pocket and plugged in her earbuds, choosing her favorite playlist to drown out the noise in her mind. The music poured into her ears like a balm to the parts of her that were too sore to deal with. With each step, her pace quickened. Soon she found herself on a trail that wound through the ranch—away from the people, the cabins, and the expectations. Her legs carried her up a small ridge, the dirt path winding around patches of sagebrush and wildflowers. She welcomed the burn in her muscles, grateful for the distraction. Yet, no matter how far she walked, the weight inside her wouldn't lift.

Just as the trail opened to a small clearing, a figure in the distance caught her attention. It leaned against a large rock, casually tossing small stones into the brush. She paused in her steps, weary of moving forward. Instinctively, she wished she hadn't gone too far without Charlie. Typically, they did hikes together. So, she was used to the shadow of protection, even in the Arizona terrains. After a moment of shifting in her shoes, wondering if she should move forward, she finally recognized who was sitting by that rock. It was Desmond, with his blond hair illuminated in the late day sunlight. Even from where she stood, the scarlet rose captured a faraway look in his hazel eyes. As if sensing another presence around him, his face was pulled in her direction. As soon as he saw her, he broke into a smile she couldn't deny. It seemed all too easy for him, as if the weight of the world had all of a sudden dropped from his shoulders, though it was there just moments ago.

"Fancy meeting you out here!" Desmond called out, waving as she approached. Ryland forced herself to pull out her earbuds and return the gesture, though her mind was still elsewhere.

"Needed some fresh air..." she admitted, trying to sound casual, though she heard the strain in her voice. "You?"

Desmond shrugged. "Same. This place can feel a bit... suffocating at times." His eyes flickered toward the ranch behind them, and Ryland sensed something deeper in his words. But he didn't elaborate. Instead, he gestured for her to join him. Without much thought, she walked over and leaned against the same rock, grateful for a moment to rest.

As she settled beside him, Desmond's eyes floated to her hand, particularly what was in it. "How'd you get that pass the Turners?" Desmond remarked, causing Ryland to follow his gaze to her phone. "Seems like you've found a loophole."

Her stomach dropped at his words. Though she tried masking it with a shrug, tucking her phone away as swift and smoothly as she could. "It helps me think," Ryland replied, though her mind was already spinning. Was there really no means of communication for anyone in this place? Come to think of it, she realized there wasn't a single sign of a landline anywhere on the ranch. Sure, they were in the middle of nowhere, but the ranch presented itself as a resort with technical advances. Plus, she still had a mobile connection, just not a strong one. Another part of her mind waved away those thoughts as irrational and downright insane. So, she chalked it up as an effort to keep couples engaged with one another. Still... it unsettled her, like an itch she couldn't quite reach.

Desmond tilted his head, as if reading the shift in her mood. "I get it," he comforted, yet there was an undertone in his words she couldn't quite put her finger on. "It's nice to escape every now and then. A part of me wonders if my efforts are actually being counted or if I'm being stalled. Or worse... *distracted.*"

Ryland swallowed hard, unsure how to react. It was as if he had been reading her thoughts all along, like an open book. She feared they were written all over her face, like he could see through the layers she'd been carefully wrapping around herself all her life. Was that it? Had she been distracted this whole time? Were all her efforts of moving forward actually leading her down an endless circle? Her mind flashed back to the moment she walked in on Charlie earlier, the packet in his hands, the way he seemed so... distant. They were supposed to be here to fix their relationship, but why did it feel like they were further apart than ever?

Desmond's voice pulled her from her thoughts. "Hey..." he said, as if attempting to reach out to her. He leaned in just slightly, his voice lowering like he was about to let her in on a secret. "A few of us are planning to slip out for a bit this weekend. Get away from all of this... therapy stuff. Clear our heads." He paused, gauging her reaction before adding, "You should come, and Charlie too. It could do you two some good."

Ryland hesitated, though her pulse quickened with both temptation and a sliver of guilt. She *wanted* to stay and work things out with Charlie. But a part of her—an ever-growing part—deeply desired reprieve. She had been trying so hard, but what was the point if everything was falling apart anyway?

She glanced at Desmond, who watched her expectantly, but not pushy. It was just an offer. No strings. No pressure.

"I'll think about it," Ryland finally said, her voice softer than before, but with a trace of resolve. Desmond smiled again, a casual nod of understanding passing between them.

"You know where to find me," he said with a wink, before pushing himself off the rock and giving her a wave as he headed down the trail.

Before she could fully grasp what just happened, he was out of sight. But not out of mind. Ryland stayed behind for a moment, her thoughts tangled. The ranch, Charlie, the Turners, a means of an escape—they all felt like different threads, pulling her in opposite directions. Too many paths with no clarity or relief from uncertainty. All she knew was that something didn't feel right, though she desperately clung to the bit of hope budding inside. But instead of confronting it, she shoved the feeling down, deep enough where she wouldn't have to deal with it—at least, just for now.

She turned back down the trail, the music in her ears once again, blocking out everything else as she walked away.

CHAPTER FOURTEEN

The sun had finally dipped behind the hills, casting long shadows across the ranch. Ryland and Charlie returned to their cabin, exhausted and more distant than ever. Charlie collapsed on the couch, still wearing the clothes he had worn all day. Ryland, though tired, forced herself through the motions of slipping into her pajamas and brushing her teeth. But when her head hit the pillow, sleep—the one thing she desperately craved—escaped her, leaving her trapped with her thoughts once again.

Her mind became a battleground, memories and worries intruding like relentless invaders. Pressing a palm against her forehead, Ryland let out a heavy groan. All she wanted was to forget—the good, the bad, and everything in between. To simply shut it all off. She squeezed her eyes shut and forced herself to sleep, fighting her own mind with a kind of desperation that left her muscles aching. For what felt like an eternity, she wrestled with her thoughts until, finally, her body surrendered to exhaustion. Her mind was the last fortress to fall, but eventually, it too gave in.

But triumph was short-lived.

Her eyes fluttered open. Frustration immediately flared within her as sunlight poured harshly through the windows. Instinctively, her hand raised to her face, shielding herself from the intensity piercing her eyes. When her eyes adjusted to the lighting of the room, her gaze shifted to the nightstand. Her eyes widened at the time flashing on the screen of a digital clock. 8:45 AM? How? Her mind reeled, searching for anything that remotely made sense. "It was just eleven at night," she muttered to herself, her voice thickened with confusion.

Her gaze shifted back to the clock. That's when she noticed what was off. It wasn't the industrial digital clock she had come to expect when she woke up on the ranch. Instead, it was the pink castle alarm clock she hadn't seen since before she left for college. It was a souvenir from her older sister Callie—a gift from her fourteenth birthday.

Memories flooded her mind all at once. Callie had brought the clock back from California when she still worked in the Disney college program. That summer of 2013 was a strain between the sisters. Ryland felt left behind to be stuck with Mama—and her unpredictable temper—in Flagstaff, while Callie escaped to California to enjoy what was left of her youth.

Ryland dug her elbows in the mattress beneath her and hauled herself upright, with her eyes scanning the room around her. Mama had divorced their father years before, scraping together what little money she had to rent a small two-bedroom apartment. The sisters shared a room, but their sides were distinct. Callie's half was decorated with pop culture memorabilia from the 2000s—posters of iconic pop stars, bright decor, and glittery knick-knacks. Ryland's side of the room was all grunge and retro, her collection of vinyl records, band tees, colorful dye to revamp the style of peekaboo highlights in her hair, and neon-colored sneakers scattered about.

Her eyes landed on the wall calendar pinned to the closet door. The first two days of July were marked with large, red Xs, which meant that it was July 3rd, 2013. It was seven days after Ryland's birthday. Seven days since Callie headed back to California. A tear slipped down Ryland's cheek as she stared at the calendar, the absence of her sister weighing heavily over her.

"Why did you have to go?" she whispered, her voice barely audible, a question that only she could hear.

Abruptly, a sharp pounding from the other side of the door jolted the scarlet rose from her thoughts. With Ryland still speechless and rattled with fear, Mama's voice boomed through the walls. "How long are you going to sleep?" she barked. "I need help with breakfast!"

Ryland squeezed her eyes closed, silently lifting a prayer to Heaven for Mama not to drive her to total insanity. Once she managed to even out her breathing, she willed herself out of bed. On her way to the door, she caught a glimpse of her reflection in the vanity mirror she shared with Callie. Her hair, which was straightened with bleached highlights at the front, fell messily around her shoulders. Her eyeliner was smudged from sleep, and she still wore her favorite black Mudhoney band T-shirt and red plaid pajama pants—an outfit her fourteen-year-old self had loved to lounge around in. But seeing herself only stirred up dread of the on-coming scorn from Mama.

As she stepped out of her room, the aroma of bacon and eggs allured her nose, but the growling of her stomach gave away her presence in the kitchen. Despite the deafening sizzles from the stove, Mama's sharp eyes were already on her, giving her the same disapproving glare as many times before. Ryland avoided her gaze, moving quietly toward the kitchen table where a pack of flour and a mixing bowl waited for her. Most of the ingredients for waffles were already laid out—sugar, milk, and butter. But...

"Are there any more eggs?" Ryland asked with a voice almost a whisper, careful not to provoke Mama any further.

Instead of the typical snippy remarks, she was redirected to the fridge without a word. Mama's back was turned as she tended to the sizzling bacon. Ryland retrieved the carton of eggs, but the momentary peace was short-lived. "So, who was that boy last night?" Mama's voice cut through the air, halting Ryland in her tracks. Her heart hit the pit of her stomach, knowing where this was going. "I saw him drop you off," her mother continued, cold and accusingly.

Ryland swallowed, her voice caught in her throat. "He's just a friend," she managed to say.

"Don't play stupid with me!" Mama snapped, her tone now crude and sharp. "I told you, no distractions! None!"

"I'm not dating him," Ryland protested weakly. "We, and some friends, caught a late showtime at the mall, and he gave me a ride home."

"Then pick an earlier movie next time!" Mama snapped, her fury simmering as she turned her attention back to the stove.

Ryland said nothing more, focusing on the task at hand—making the waffles. She measured everything carefully, determined to get it right. But the earlier confrontation replayed in her mind, blurring any effort of concentration. Her heart pounded in her ears, as she mixed the batter, trying to shake off the feeling of failure that clung to her.

Mindlessly, she turned away from the counter, mixing bowl in hand. At the same time, Mama turned away from the stove. Before either of the two could stop themselves, a collision erupted in the kitchen. Batter was all over the floor along with Mama and Ryland covered in some of it. In the flashing moment, she was knocked to the ground with her cheek in her palm. Tears stung her eyes as Mama's slur of anger rang in her ears.

"Why are you so space-headed? Look what you did!" Mama screamed. "That's why I don't let you touch anything! You break everything!"

Ryland stood there, frozen in place, as Mama continued her tirade. Batter clung to her clothes, her cheek burning from the slap, but the pain was nothing compared to the shame that consumed her. Without another word, she fled to her room, slamming the door behind her and locking it. She still heard Mama from the kitchen, but she no longer cared.

She sank to the floor, leaning against the door as her body trembled with sobs. "How much longer do I have to stay here?" she muttered. Her mind screamed, Stop! Stop! Stop!

"Ryland! Get out here now!"

"No!" escaped Ryland's lips as she bolted upright. The moonlight streamed through the windows as she found herself back in the cabin. She glanced over her shoulder, longing for comfort, but Charlie's side of the bed was still left undisturbed. Tears spewed out of her like a leak from a broken cistern. Her bones jangled uncontrollably as she sobbed with her face collapsed in her hands. Salt-soaked fear slid down her wrists as she curled into a ball. She didn't hear the soft footsteps approaching nor did she jerk as his familiar arms wrapped around her. She didn't have to look up. His hair fell around her like a curtain of protection, and his cheek rested gently against hers. Ryland leaned into his embrace, her tears building a pool in her hands as Charlie held her close.

"It's okay…" he cooed. "I'm here… I'm always here."

CHAPTER FIFTEEN

The weekend finally arrived, offering Ryland and Charlie reprieve from being probed and needled by speculations of their counselors and the exhausting efforts of constant socializing. The ranch—though once idyllic—had become tense with a growing estrangement between them. But that Friday fell on the couple like a small relief of rain on their desert lands. They finally found a pocket of peace in the midst of chaos plaguing their minds. Although Charlie had become more weary of the scarlet rose, and Ryland sensed it. It was like every move of a muscle or a twitch of her nose invoked a silent, "Are you okay?" She couldn't blame him. Neither of the two had been the same since that night she dreamt of Mama. With all their years together, Charlie had never seen her like that before. Not until then. Somehow, the hand of grace pulled them back together when they decided to try out archery, one of the activities on their bucket list since joining the ranch. Unexpectedly, it rekindled something between them. Laughter filled the air, in fullness and unburdened, as they playfully challenged each other. Delicately, the tension between them dissolved by every moment.

By nightfall, the couple crawled into bed with well-earned exhaustion. As her eyes fluttered closed, Ryland found herself cocooned in the comfort of Charlie's arms. The warmth of his embrace followed her as she slipped into REM without the claws of ephialtes holding her hostage. For the first time in days, her heart found solace in the quiet assurance that maybe, just maybe, they could find their way back to each other.

The next morning, the couple remained in a sweet mood. Ryland couldn't help but savor Charlie's soft, adoring gazes. He guided her to the back porch, where a patio set matched the earthy tones of the landscape. From their seats, they marveled at the view of the lake, which stretched into the distance. It was a picturesque blue beneath a sky adorned with fluffy ivory clouds. Lush wildflowers and vibrant cacti surrounded the lake, their vivid colors painting the ground with a splash of life.

Ryland pulled away from the scene and glanced at Charlie, wondering what he was thinking. But his gaze hadn't left her. She extended her hand, allowing his to slip over hers. Sparked by his touch, her heart fluttered. Oh how much she missed this closeness. For a second, she thought, *Maybe this was all I needed...*

Charlie, sensing her racing inclinations, was about to say something when a faint knock interrupted them. They dismissed it at first, assuming it was just the house settling. Then the sound came again, more persistent. Charlie—overtaken by curiosity—hopped out his chair and ducked back inside. A few more moments passed when Ryland finally heard his voice carry back to her ears, but it was followed by a voice she quickly recognized. She, too, left the porch on the mission to figure out what was holding him. As soon as she stepped inside, she found Charlie chatting with Sabrina at the door. It didn't take long for the awareness of his fiancée to direct his attention to her. He reached out an arm, inviting her to join them, which *she* happily accepted.

As Ryland approached the pair, she noted Sabrina's return to her usual style. Her sleek raven-colored bob was pinned back, allowing her sterling teardrop earrings to glimmer in the late morning light. She wore a white lace tank top that hugged her torso and a denim skirt held up by a silver concho chain belt, paired with black ankle booties. A glossy smile brightened her face as soon as she saw Ryland.

"Hey!" Ryland greeted her. "What's going on?"

"I was wondering if you two wanted to hang out with me and some friends today," Sabrina offered. "We're about to head out in a bit."

Ryland perked up, immediately reminded of Desmond's earlier invitation. "Oh, um... I'd love to, but Desmond kind of invited Charlie and me already. I told him we'd join him."

Sabrina laughed. "Uh, he invited you to hang out with *us*."

"Oh..." Ryland grinned sheepishly, glancing at Charlie. "I don't mind."

Charlie smiled and said, "I'd love an escape for the day."

His words might have stung Ryland, but she had to admit the same. The ranch was starting to wear on her. A change of scenery sounded perfect, and she wanted to hold on to what felt like bliss between her and Charlie. Sabrina mentioned the group would leave in thirty minutes, giving the couple just enough time to get ready.

Ryland ditched the ranch's uniform of flannel and plain jeans and turned to her wardrobe for inspiration. From her personal collection, she plucked out a fitted brown T-shirt and a cream-colored cargo skirt. After defining her long curls with some mousse, she pinned the frontal tresses behind her ears with a few bobby pins. She added small gold hoops, a matching arm bangle, and slid on a pair of apricot snip-toe booties. Slinging a matching crossbody purse over one shoulder, she stepped out of the room. Charlie spun around at the sound of her footsteps, his gaze locking onto her.

It never took long for him to get ready. With his easygoing aura and bohemian style, Charlie could pull off anything without much effort. Ryland had always envied his self-assurance, but when he looked at her, his expression softened in admiration.

Ryland had to admit, she almost felt like her old self again.

For a moment, they stood there, face to face, gazing at one another. Ryland wondered what had gotten into them. Even, for a moment, she questioned why they were on the ranch in the first place. The longer she held his gaze, the more the entire thing seemed futile. She almost voiced these thoughts, but Charlie took her by the hand and led her out the door.

The couple followed in the direction Sabrina instructed before she left them to get ready. The path evidently led to Charlie's Silverado, which was seemingly untouched since he last attended it. As soon as he saw it, he quickened his pace to check on it. Ryland, on the other hand, froze in her tracks as her attention was drawn to the vehicle sitting next to the Silverado.

That truck was back.

Sabrina sat on the hood while Desmond leaned against the front, his back facing Ryland. A few yards away stood Cheyenne, Xavier, and Tathia. Cheyenne and Xavier were deep in conversation with a guy Ryland didn't recognize. Even while cross-legged on the ground, she could tell he was quite lengthy in stature, possibly matching Charlie's height. His dark brown hair was chopped in a buzzcut, though it accentuated his sharp jaw and urban style. He wore a solid black short-sleeve shirt, which was paired with grey camouflage pants, and starkly contrasted his creamy complexion. Resting on his shoulder was Tathia as she sported a flirty blush pink dress that barely touched the knees. Her ombre honey hair was no longer in her typical high-ponytail but spilled freely down one shoulder, exposing a dazzling set of earrings that matched her dress.

As Ryland approached the scene, she overheard Xavier's question, "Are they coming?" prompting Sabrina to glance around.

It wasn't long before her eyes spotted his answer. As Ryland drew near, Sabrina exclaimed, "Oh, hi!". Then she gave the scarlet rose a onceover, confusion faltering her grin. "Where's Charlie?"

Ryland pointed to the Silverado as his familiar voice called out. The other faces brightened at the sight of the couple. Cheyenne and Tathia immediately pulled Ryland into their arms, flickering a warmth she hadn't felt before. She peeked over their shoulders at Charlie, who quickly re-bonded with Desmond and Xavier. She drank in the way his grin danced on his face as his hair floated behind him in the wind. He was like a total school boy with his pals as they playfully scuffled a bit and cracked some jokes, followed by Desmond's bellowed laugh in the serene afternoon air.

Sabrina's voice yanked back to the trio standing before her. "Are you two all set? We'll be out all day."

Ryland nodded. "Yeah, we're good."

"Great! Let's get out of here before my parents or one of their bootlickers catch us," Sabrina teased.

Ryland blinked, caught off guard by the remark. She wanted to ask what Sabrina meant, but before she could,

Sabrina had already gathered the others. Desmond mentioned they had room in his truck for Ryland and Charlie, but the couple opted to drive the Silverado instead, promising to stay close behind.

As they settled into their car, each touch of the familiar leather seats sparked an on slot of sentiments they had built between them. Ryland watched Charlie place his hands on the steering wheel. With his eyes lingered on it for a moment, she caught something flickering in them—sadness or nostalgia, perhaps? She reached out, softly placing her hand on his shoulder. That seemed to jerk him awake from his thoughts just in time to see their friends fleeting down the road. Without a word, Charlie ignited the engine and quickly closed the gap between them.

After about a fifteen-mile drive, a gas station popped into view. Charlie let out a cheer, grateful for the stop as he had been eyeing the fuel gauge warily. As soon as both vehicles came to a halt, the group dispersed. Xavier headed for the restroom, the girls made a beeline for the mini-market, while Desmond and Charlie stayed behind to assess their cars. Ryland checked in with Charlie before following the girls, but he waved her off, assuring her that he was just fine. "Go have fun," he nudged, then kissed her forehead.

Inside, the girls browsed the aisles, chatting away. In the middle of Tathia's search for relationship advice, something *she* said sparked a craving for cereal in Cheyenne. Tathia decided to accompany their friend, as a sweet tooth of her own crept on her tongue, leaving Ryland and Sabrina alone by the magazine rack. Ryland flipped through a circular, skimming an article about another Hollywood divorce, when Sabrina's voice broke the silence.

"I can't wait until I finally get married..." she muttered wistfully. Her voice was so low, Ryland almost thought she wasn't meant to hear that.

Still, she encouraged, "I'm sure you will someday."

Sabrina glanced at the redhead, curiosity and excitement electrifying her eyes.

That's when Ryland spotted a bridal magazine in the young Turner's hands. "My sister always believed that the desires we have were given to us for a reason," the scarlet rose added.

"Really? Do you think it's in the cards for me?" Sabrina asked, her voice hopeful.

Ryland smiled and nodded.

"I've wished for it since I was six years old," Sabrina said. "I remember, one day, I found my mom's wedding gown in this beautiful porcelain box she kept in her wardrobe. It was pearly white, made of satin and lace. She caught me, too, but it was then I learned about their love story. It was so cliche, but I kind of want that."

Ryland's heart was moved by such a charming confession. She let herself picture the young Turner gliding down the aisle in that pearly white dress. But this thought begged the question, "Are you in a relationship?" Just like that, sadness rushed into Sabrina's eyes like a high tide crashing on halcyon shores, as if Ryland's question broke through the dam in her mind. For the first time, the young Turner was actually lost for words. She hesitated before her gaze drifted to the windows, where the boys were still chatting. Ryland followed her gaze, landing on Desmond. "How long has it been?"

Sabrina let out a soft, melancholic chuckle. "My parents broke us up... or at least, they *think* they did. We just make sure they don't see us together."

Ryland's eyes widened. "Why would they do that? Aren't you, what, twenty?"

"Twenty-two," Sabrina corrected with a sad smile. "They didn't approve of Desmond. I should've known better than to invite him to dinner. When he asked for my hand, they shut him down immediately. Apparently, a male nurse isn't good enough for them."

Ryland scoffed. "People still believe in that?"

Sabrina shrugged. "My parents do."

Ryland shook her head, but hearing that took her back to Mama's disapproval of Charlie. Familiar determination tingled on her tongue as she said half to herself, "Maybe you could move out…"

But a laugh escaped Sabrina so dark and tender that it tore Ryland to see such hopelessness in those young eyes. She wanted to promise the young Turner that escape was possible, but the scarlet rose was bombarded with Sabrina's next words. "By the way, I saw how you eyed Desmond's truck," she pointed out, locking her green eyes on the redhead. Her countenance returned to its radiant state as that bouncy tone resurfaced in her voice. "You would've thought it tried to eat you…"

Ryland nearly flinched, thrown off by the sudden shift. Soon, she recovered, recognizing Sabrina's defenses. "It may not have tried to eat me," she refuted, "but it did almost run Charlie and me off the road."

Sabrina's face twisted with brows furrowed, earnestly puzzled by such a remark. Ryland explained what had happened, and by the end of it, Sabrina was shaking her head, sighing. "I keep telling Xavier to stop doing that."

"What?"

"Xavier's a bit of a daredevil," Sabrina admitted. "He likes to prank people on the road whenever Desmond lets him drive. I'm sorry he scared you—I had no idea it was you and Charlie that night."

Hit with shock, Ryland found that hard to swallow. She expected a confrontation, but it was deeper than that. It was the first time she was understood, let alone getting an apology.

Sabrina placed a hand on her shoulder, her eyes sincere. "We're still okay, right?"

Ryland gave a soft nod, reassuring the young Turner.

The girls were then regrouped when Cheyenne and Tathia returned with boxes of cereal and candy. They paid for their items and headed back outside to join the boys. Tathia's fiancé, Jared, asked if they were ready to hit the road again. Tathia, flashing a glossy grin, bantered, "I've waited too long for Pink Soundscapes to miss it."

As Tathia spoke, Xavier eyed his wife curiously. He pointed to the box of cereal tucked under her arm, as she munched on a scoopful. "Are those fruity flavored?" he asked. Cheyenne bobbed her head like a kid after ransacking a candy store, then handed him the box. It didn't take long before he had a handful in his mouth too.

With that, the group folded back into their respective cars.

Both vehicles were back on the road, trekking down the highways in the direction of the music festival. As Charlie drove, his hand reached for Ryland's. She let him interlock his fingers with hers, as every touch sparked a refreshing warmth in her. She glanced at him, though his eyes remained on the road. She didn't mind. In fact, she missed the feeling of trusting him wherever they went. For the first time, she didn't care at all about a destination. She simply wanted to enjoy the journey.

CHAPTER FIFTEEN

Ryland's boots sank into the cool, damp grass as she and Charlie stepped into the landscape of Pink Soundscapes. The air was sweet with candied almonds and faint whiffs of lavender, swirling with a trace of humidity. Festival flags billowed overhead like pastel banners, catching the warm wind, while the low hum of a bass guitar vibrated through the grounds, mingling with the chatter of the crowds weaving through tents, booths, and stages. The melodic ambiance of acoustic and electric guitars, distant drums, and murmurings of voices surrounded them like the quiet rush of a stream.

She could already feel a slow unfurling inside her. It was a quiet joy that budded in her chest and spread, thawing out the cold places buried so deep. Instinctively, Ryland squeezed Charlie's hand, feeling his warmth seeping into her palm. Charlie glanced at her, flashing a tender smile. "Doesn't this remind you of our road trip to Coachella?" he said, a low chuckle escaping him.

Giggling, Ryland also recalled that trip with their friends in college. It was their own getaway to celebrate the last few weeks of senior year. She could almost still hear their favorite songs blasting through the dashboard speakers as they took on the five-hour drive to Indio. But back then was nothing compared to now, with Charlie. Even with their new friends mingling about, Ryland was glad to finally have him all to herself. Her senses heightened in the backdrop of dream pop serenading them, like a soundtrack to their memories.

Turning to Charlie, she mentioned, "Remember that weird café we found with the guitars hanging on the walls? The owner claimed he used to play with AC/DC."

Charlie rolled his head back at the memory. "Oh yeah! Perrie actually believed him!"

"His Steely Dan collection was a dead giveaway," quipped Ryland.

Though Charlie relished the faux pas of their friend, he added, "I have to admit... It was a neat rack."

Ryland snorted as they bypassed a vendor selling caramel popcorn and hot dogs. "Deep Purple any day..." She even missed doing that with Charlie—having endless debates about bands and their decades-old classics.

"Okay, but if you could only listen to one band for a full year, would it be Styx or Rush?" Charlie challenged, a triumphant grin dancing on his cheeks as they walked deeper into the heart of the festival.

Ryland could hear a new song playing, different from the one she originally heard when they first walked through the entrance of the venue. This time, it was a gentle symphony with haunting overtones echoing from a nearby stage. She recognized this ballad as it stirred something deeper inside her. The closer she listened, she was slowly led back to that day when Charlie took her to their favorite lake and got down on one knee. She remembered how beautiful he looked in the moonlight as the perfectly picked marquise diamond ring glistened in the silver streams. Ryland almost forgot that he was standing right next to her, waiting for an answer.

"Oh, um... that's a tough choice," she tried to respond as quickly as possible, but her mind was already far gone. "How about you?"

"Rush," Charlie said almost too fast.

Ryland scrunched her nose. That was enough to grab her attention. "I always thought you were more of a Styx guy..."

They maneuvered through clusters of people, passing booths selling handmade jewelry that glittered in the sunlight. There were also art pieces that bled colors onto canvases in abstract beauty. Ryland felt Charlie's hand tighten around hers as they walked by an old vinyl stall, the scent of well-worn records causing her heart to skip.

Charlie lowered closer to her ear. "Look at that," he murmured, pointing to a more visible rack.

Ryland followed his gaze to an album cover she recognized immediately—a striking blend of blush and lilac, a perfect storm of nostalgia. "Hounds of Love!" she chirped at the sight of their favorite Kate Bush record.

"Yep!" Charlie affirmed, his eyes twinkling. The couple played that entire album on their first date, and the night he proposed. Although, the evoking lyrics of "Watching You Without Me" snuck into that moment of reminiscing together. She was drawn back to the present when Charlie slipped his arm around her and gently pulled her close. "I'm telling you, it's like we were born in the wrong year."

"Eh, 1999 had its highlights," Ryland jibed. "Britney Spears, the Y2K Apocalypse..." she proceeded to list, with the last part erupting a hearty laugh from Charlie's chest.

"Okay, even for you, that was a bit dark," he jabbed at her.

She shrugged and strutted to his words like a pageant queen. "Yeah, well... I'm full of surprises..."

The two of them continued to meander through the grounds, taking in the sights and sounds. There was something about Pink Soundscapes—the colors, the music, the vibrancy—that made it feel as though time had folded in on itself. They relished in this version of their relationship that felt untouched and uncomplicated, as if the weight of the days before had been blotted out and tossed into oblivion. Ryland sipped every last drop as their adventurous souls reconnected, laughing more than they fought and believing that love could hold them together through anything.

At one of the smaller stages, a new band was setting up, tuning their guitars as the crowd slowly gathered. That's when Ryland remembered their friends. She glanced about, looking for them, but the crowd was innumerable. No face remotely appeared familiar. Just as she was about to raise this concern to Charlie, the lead singer whispered a beautifully melancholic tune, stirring a tumultuous praise across the crowd. Ryland couldn't help but feel drawn to her voice too. After a few notes, the sound dropped, evoking a strained yet calculated pause. The crowd waited as tensions built, until a smile flashed across the singer's face. Abruptly, the drums pounded something sonic, followed by bassier beats and a guitar riff. The stunt pulled together into something raw and alluring. The crowd went wild. As the melody weaved through her ears, Ryland succumbed to it like a landslide. Eventually, she decided to let herself be at ease and enjoy dancing and singing along.

The couple stayed for the entire set, which lasted about half an hour. Then, Charlie—who never dropped her hand—guided her away from the crowd until they found a quiet spot nestled in the shade of a large oak tree. Charlie lay back on the grass, his arms folded beneath his head. Ryland sat beside him, her knees drawn to her chest. For a while, they just let the music fill the spaces between them. The wind tugged gently at her crimson ringlets as she ran her fingers through them absentmindedly, watching as the leaves above them swayed in the breeze.

Then, Charlie's voice slipped through the halcyon atmosphere. "I missed this."

Ryland glanced down at him, her heart catching in her throat. She knew what he meant. Not just the festival or the road adventures, but the way they used to be. Carefree. Untangled by the knots of life. She wanted to admit the same thing, but the other part that was left at the ranch still clung to her. Her eyes drifted back toward the stage, where a new artist had taken over.

Charlie shifted, propping himself fully upright with the help of his elbows, but his gaze remained fixed on her. "Do we have to go back?" His words touched her ears so endearingly, laced with a faint plea that crushed her all over again.

"Charlie..."

"I *dread* going back there." Waving his hand between himself and the scarlet rose, he added, "I don't want to lose this."

Ryland's heart clenched at the thought. "It's not that simple," she said softly, her voice tinged with regret. "We can't just... I can't run away from everything."

Befuddled, his brows knitted as the wheels in his mind spun, attempting to grasp her words. "Running away from what?" he questioned. "Is that what this is about?" Ryland didn't respond but looked away, fighting back the tears stinging her eyes. He placed his hand on her shoulder, trying his best to soothe her pain despite not knowing how. "Dove, what are you running away from?"

Ryland couldn't bring herself to look at him. He called out to her, but by this point, the tears were rolling down her face. He threw his arms around her and let her head rest on his chest. "I'm sorry," he said. "I think I've been a bit worn out. It wasn't my intent to upset you."

But that wasn't it. If only she could simply tell him how much of a burden she felt—that she had entangled him in a mess that wasn't his to begin with.

Both Ryland and Charlie fell silent again, allowing the scarlet rose to gather herself. Her dark-haired beau caressed her cheek, which seemed to balm her aching mind. Ryland peered up at him, wondering what he was thinking at that moment, but his eyes were drawn elsewhere. She traced his stare back to the animated crowds. Suddenly, she heard the music all around them again. Charlie's face lit up with that boyish grin she adored. Without another word, he stood up, pulling the fiery-haired darling to her feet. "Come on," he said with sparkling eyes. "I have an idea."

They weaved their way through the festival grounds again with hands intertwined. They passed food trucks offering artisanal pizzas and gourmet ice cream, more art booths showcasing hand-painted murals, and jewelry made from recycled material. Every corner of the festival seemed to hum with life and creativity, and Ryland found herself swept away in the abundance of excitement again. It was like she had stepped into a new dream.

Then they ended up in a spot where a small, intimate stage was tucked beneath a canopy of trees. Floating from the stage and into their ears were the soft, ethereal tunes of a solo guitarist tenderly plucking each string. Ryland hadn't realized how long they had been out and about until she caught a glimpse of the setting sun casting a golden glow over everything. She all but swooned at how its rays spilled into the deep sienna pools of Charlie's eyes. He pulled Ryland close, wrapping his arms around his scarlet rose as they began to sway gently to the song. Ryland rested her head against his chest, her eyes closing as she let the twinkling strings and the steady rhythm of his heartbeat wash over her.

For a while, they didn't speak. There was no need. The music, the setting, the warmth of his arms around her said more than words ever could. But right when it felt like they could last forever, Sabrina's pitchy voice sliced through the moment. "Guys, I found them!" Just like that, their peaceful world was shattered as reality flooded in.. Soon enough, the young couple were surrounded by familiar faces, reminding them where they had to go back to eventually.

Cheyenne bolted forward, her eyes trembling. "We were looking all over for you!" she cried, exasperated from the group's widespread search. "Are you two okay?"

Ryland and Charlie exchanged looks as their nerves kicked up. Looking back at their friends, Charlie replied, "We were just walking around."

"We figured you guys were doing the same," added Ryland. "Although I was a bit worried we might've lost you."

Desmond let out a whistle, as Xavier remarked, "You sure know how to explore because you two went *deep!*"

Ryland flashed an apologetic grin. "Sorry, it's kind of our thing."

"Clearly..." teased Jared, as he held Tathia close.

Sabrina rolled her eyes at their friends but directed her concern at Ryland and Charlie. "We have to get back to the ranch..." she said. "I forgot that today is the third Saturday of the month. My parents like to pull me into these dinner parties they throw for their rich friends. If they realize I'm gone, we're toast!"

That sinking feeling weighed on Ryland again, like a stone yanking her quickly to the bottom of the ocean. What was that supposed to mean? What would happen if they got caught? She turned to Charlie, whose eyes went dark with an emotion she didn't recognize. Without a word from either of them, the couple followed their friends out of the venue and back to their cars, doing everything they could to race against time.

CHAPTER SIXTEEN

The couple and their friends made it back in the knick of time. As soon as both cars touched base, Sabrina gave her quick goodbyes before flying down the dirt path toward her parents' house. Ryland and Charlie said their goodbyes to the rest of the group and made their way back to their cabin. The walk there was in complete silence between the scarlet rose and her fiancé, though it wasn't unbearable. Ryland was able to rest on that journey back with Charlie. At the same time, the fear in Sabrina's eyes haunted Ryland, but not more than the things the young Turner told her. Her mind's eye brought up how she felt when she still lived with Mama—entrapped and suffocated.

As Charlie and Ryland neared their cabin, a couple of voices arose. Ryland couldn't make out what was being said, but she quickly sensed the pent-up tension darkening the serenity around them. Her brown eyes scanned the perimeter for any possible source of those disembodied voices. But it wasn't long before she found what she was looking for.

A man and a woman—middle-aged and worn out from the day—stood face to face, red and emotional. A slur of harshness spilled from their lips like foam, and their eyes were heightened and adrenalized. Ryland froze in her tracks, preventing Charlie from moving forward. He followed where her attention was pulled. Ryland was taken aback by her recognition of the couple. It was Adam and Lydia. As their testimonies replayed in her ears, she saw tears spilling down Lydia's face. Adam had ditched the flannel for an outfit that seemed more personal to him, and hanging on his shoulders was an army-green backpack filled to the brim. *Is he about to walk away?* This thought flashed across Ryland's mind.

Just as she turned in their direction, though not entirely sure what she could possibly do, Charlie guided her away from any attempt she had in mind. "Let's go," he prompted, his arm around her. "That's something they have to sort out on their own."

"But—" Ryland tried to protest, but Charlie had already pulled them both inside their cabin.

As soon as he closed the door behind him, he faced Ryland, his stare cautious and tentative. "The one thing I'm beginning to understand," he began, "is that the relationship you have with someone stays between them and you. Not everyone's advice has the right intentions. And even if their heart is in the right place, it doesn't mean their advice is profitable." He paused, combing his fingers through the roots of his dark tresses and staying that way for a moment. Ryland reached her hand out to him, letting it rest on the upper part of his arm. "A part of me thinks that's what they might be dealing with right now...." he finally said, as if trying to confess something. Ryland wanted to pry into his mind, but what if she found exactly what the other part of her feared? Instead of taking up that fight, the scarlet rose put her armor down. She kissed him goodnight, suggested he get some sleep, and then headed for bed.

But inklings still haunted her for the rest of the weekend. By Monday morning, she was back to her old habit of being trapped in her mind.

After attending the group session, Ryland headed to her meeting with Breanna. As she stepped inside the counselor's whimsical cabin, the bouncy brunette met her by the door. "Hey, kiddo!" she greeted, placing a gentle hand on Ryland's arm. But the scarlet rose was keenly aware of something hidden in the brunette's shifty blue eyes. "I know we're supposed to have our time today... but Sherrie decided that you should meet with her."

It took all her strength to keep up the nonchalant facade, but a storm of bewilderment and dread flooded into her as Sabrina came to mind. *Did Sherrie find out?*

Nonetheless, Ryland thanked Breanna for letting her know before making her way up the hill to the Turner house. Before she could knock on the door, it flew open, revealing Sherrie, who apparently expected the red-haired darling. She was led to a different office than the one she recalled from her initial visit to the Turner estate. This office was decorated with monochrome schemes. There was a three-seat couch made of onyx leather, which leaned against the wall near the entrance of the office, and faced Sherrie's oak-wooden desk. Her desk was surrounded by shelves that showcased peer-reviewed journals of almost all topics and houses of thought in the psychology realm. Some rows within the shelves were accented with knick knacks and Sherrie's trophies. On her desk was a rose-gold laptop neatly placed in the center with an open notebook sitting on the left side of it. Sitting on the corner of her desk, but visible for her guest to see, was a glass plaque with her name engraved on it. Written underneath her name was the title: LICENSED CLINICAL & COUNSELING PRACTITIONER.

Ryland plotted herself on the couch, sitting particularly in the middle, as Sherrie found her place behind her desk. As the Turner settled in her chair, her straight raven tresses swayed, lightly brushing against the square neck collar of her denim dress. Her red bangles rattled against the surface of her desk as she started typing on the keyboard. Then, she grabbed a pen from a marble holder, which rested near her plaque, and pulled her notebook closer to her. Looking up at the scarlet rose, who watched her curiously, Sherrie's eyes sparkled at the sight of her. But Ryland caught something else behind them.

"I know you're probably freaking out with me summoning you here," she joked. "But I just wanted to catch up and see how you were handling the program so far, especially with us being halfway through our two-week agreement."

Ryland was relieved to hear that. So, she shuffled away all thoughts of Sabrina and the weekend. "Thanks. Um... where should we start?"

Sherrie shrugged and gestured at her. "Anywhere you like."

Well, that narrows things down, she scoffed to herself. Aloud, she muttered an "Okay...". It took a moment of shuffling through her mind for the right things to say. She wasn't entirely sure what Sherrie was looking for, weary of giving too much away. As soon as she thought this, what Charlie said last night crept in her ears. She tried to wave away all manner of hesitation but it clung to the back of her mind. So, as a starter, Ryland offered, "Charlie and I have been growing closer lately."

Sherrie's brows raised but the spark in her eyes quieted. "Oh..." was her response. Then she clicked her pen and hovered it over the notebook, still eyeing Ryland. "Tell me how that's going."

"It's been quite... healing," Ryland started to explain. "I didn't realize how many things I missed about us."

That grabbed Sherrie's attention. She paused mid-writing, tilting her head, as if saying "Aww." "You two always seem so close," she remarked. "In fact, compared to all the couples Maxwell and I have been counseling, it's like you two are inseparable. I'm starting to worry..." She attempted a laugh with that last sentence.

But this tugged at Ryland, whose brow twitched at the inclination in Sherrie's voice. There were many reasons to raise an argument. It was just days before that the young couple felt so far from one another. Every word and intent seemed misunderstood on both sides. At the same time, it was comforting to hear that, on some level, their relationship still had fight left in it.

She raked her mind for a tactful reply but Sherrie beat her to it. "*So,* what are some things you felt have brought you two closer?" she inquired. "*If* you don't mind sharing, of course..."

As much as Ryland wanted to hide it, a small smile grew into a wide grin of victory as she replayed the scenes of her and Charlie in each other's arms, slowly swaying to the tunes that perfumed the weekend between them, and the way Charlie's gaze lingered on her. "Everything..." she spilled out, almost in a daze. "I don't think it was the need for anything new. We just had to remember where we came from. At least, I think that's what it was."

But Sherrie protested. "It's never good to live in the past, Ryland," she rebutted. "Create *new* memories. Always look ahead."

To an extent, Ryland had to agree. She did want something new for her and Charlie. But what if she had the wrong perspective this entire time? "What if it's not living in the past?" Ryland ventured. "What if it's the need to keep pushing forward that's actually been distracting us? How can we have a stable future if we never take a moment to appreciate the building blocks? What if it's constantly keeping an eye on a vision that causes discord?"

Sherrie chuckled, but Ryland thought she heard a sneer in her tone. "Or maybe something is hindering you from growing and that's just you trying to make sense of it instead of *getting rid of it*?"

Ryland squinted her eyes at the Turner, uncertain of where she was leading with that. "What do you mean?" she quizzed. "What could be holding me back?"

"Do you and Charlie ever talk about the future?"

At first, the scarlet rose fell silent as those words weaved through her mind. But, as they trickled in, the answer became clear. "How could we not?" she contested. "We're getting married in four weeks."

Sherrie shook her head, presumptuously. "I don't mean *wedding planning*," she clarified. "Where do you see yourselves in five years? Maybe even a year from now?"

"Oh, we've had many of those conversations," Ryland explained with a shrug. "The latest one between us started back a year ago before Charlie proposed. We've been figuring out what kind of parents we want to be."

Sherrie's brows raised, nearly touching her hairline. "Hmm..." was all she said. No other words were exchanged between the two as Sherrie wrote more in her notebook. Ryland started to wonder about the things that were possibly being penned. Before she could even hint at her doubts, Sherrie resumed the conversation. "Don't you think it's a bit soon to talk about children?"

Ryland scrunched her nose, tsk-ing at such a remark. "Charlie and I grew up estranged from our parents," she articulated. Then Ryland went on. "Charlie and his adopted parents have been for some time. I never wanted to go home, and moved out as soon as I was able to. So, Charlie and I have vowed to be a warm place for our children—a refuge they could run to—even when they're fifty."

But Sherrie shuffled in her seat as a quaint look writhed in her eyes. "And what's your sense of a good home for a child?"

Ryland's jaw clenched as something about that question stung like a knife in her heart. She almost heard Mama's voice. It sparked something in her she thought was lost. But it didn't last. Still, Ryland mustered enough courage to say, "For one—faith. The only time I've ever felt remotely close to God was Sunday morning. Even then, I couldn't focus on anything but the fear of going back home to a mom who resembled nothing the Bible taught." Hearing herself say that pierced her. She dropped her head but not the strength in her voice. "Since being with Charlie, I realized that's what I want. I want my kids to know what genuine love feels like. The kind that God teaches."

Ryland watched as Sherrie seemed to recoil, as if grasping for words that were long lost. Nothing came out. So, she put down her pen and closed her notebook. "I think we can end the session for now..." she said flatly. "Before you go, I want you to leave with this in mind... Figure out what you truly want—something outside of Charlie."

It was her turn to be lost for words. All she could do was stare at Sherrie, utterly confused about what the goal was at this point. For the first time, she was wary of Sherrie's advice. Instead of trying to make sense of it, Ryland rose to her feet and headed out of the office, finding herself in that state of bleakness all over again.

CHAPTER SEVENTEEN

The scarlet rose stepped inside the cabin with a new goal: distract, distract, distract. She needed anything to escape her mind, which was becoming more of a horrifying slideshow.

But as she walked into the living room, her ears captured the sound of water running at high speed. It traveled from the closed bathroom door, which stood opposite the entrance of their cabin. At first, she almost tuned out the water—until another sound broke through. It was faint but distinct. As she drew near the closed bathroom door, that particular sound persisted. She heard dissonant sniffles and moans, causing her heart to hit the floor. *Was that Charlie?* her mind alarmed her. Ryland lifted her hand and rapped her knuckles against the door. She called out to him, hoping for an immediate answer. But she didn't get one. She knocked again.

"Charlie!" she called out louder.

The sounds stopped short. She heard a few splashes, then the water abruptly switched off. The door jingled a bit, prompting Ryland to realize that it was locked. She stepped back, anticipating what she was about to see.

The door slowly opened, revealing Charlie with the skin on his face damp, along with the roots of his hair. His cheeks were flushed yet managed to lift into a grin, though it was half-hearted. "Hey..." he greeted, his voice small and raspy. "I didn't think you'd be back so soon."

Ryland was tempted to question him as her gaze flickered to the bathroom, searching for an answer or some kind of clue. But all she saw was a dark bathroom, partially lit by the sunlight floating in from the living room windows. So she retrained her eyes on Charlie. "I visited Sherrie today. She wanted me to have a session with her instead of Breanna."

The corners of his eyes twitched at the sound of Sherrie's name. "Oh..." was all he said. He moved around her and headed for their bedroom. So she followed him there. Charlie was already searching through their closet, from which he plucked out a simple white t-shirt and a light blue denim jacket. Ryland realized then that the chest area of his dark green button-up shirt was soaked. A new set of alarm bells went off.

"Are you okay?" she asked him.

He froze midway through trading his button-down for the t-shirt he had picked out. An odd look surfaced in his eyes, but Ryland couldn't piece it together. As quickly as it came, the look in his eyes disappeared. He resumed his outfit change. Now wearing the t-shirt, he tossed the button-down back in the closet, then slipped on his denim jacket. He pulled his long tresses into a loose bun, with a few shorter strands falling around his face. "So, how was it?" he asked, turning the tables on her.

Ryland shook her head, puzzled by the sudden shift. "How was what?"

Confusion flashed across his face as he planted himself at the edge of their bed. "You mentioned that Sherrie wanted to meet with you..."

"Oh... right..." was all Ryland could say. She studied his every move, trying to calculate the wheels churning in his head. No matter how hard she tried, it was like the wall he'd built was impenetrable. She plopped herself next to him intentionally, though feeling slightly defeated.

"It was a fair session," she started to tell him. "She just wanted to see how we were doing so far. You know, evaluating how the program has been working for us."

Charlie glanced away from her, his attention suddenly drawn to his rings, which he shifted between his fingers. "Mmm... So, what'd you say?"

Ryland gave the thought a shrug, though still canvassing him. "The truth. We finally got back to a good place lately."

But he shot her a knowing look. "Not because of the program."

Ryland let out a strained sigh, losing all will to fight. So, she decided to redirect the conversation. "Did you meet with Tyler?"

Charlie shook his head. "Oddly enough... I was with Maxwell," he mentioned. "I actually wished to be with Tyler today." Her brows knitted as a poisonous blend of conflict and curiosity dripped inside the scarlet rose.

Before Ryland could say anything, Charlie continued. "I'm telling you, since we got here, it's like I'm being dissected," he said. "Just poked and prodded until they find the right button to push." His head hung as his voice started to trail off. But as he spoke his next words, it felt as though he'd been slammed into a wall. "I'm certain they're about to find it."

Her heart softened for him. She leaned close, readily offering her shoulder. "What did he say to you?"

Charlie's eyes squeezed shut as his breath brimmed his lips, spilling slowly and burdened. "The other day, I told Tyler a bit about my parents," he began, "and I brought up Liya." Ryland's eyes widened because he never talked about his sister. The last time Liya was brought up in conversation, Ryland knew to never cross that line again.

Though she was also overcome with joy. "You talked about her on your own?" she beamed.

But this bit of blitheness was quickly shot down.

"There was no reason for her to be brought up," he asserted, "but it happened. I thought it was confidential, but Tyler told Maxwell, saying he was concerned about me and how I'm not growing. So Maxwell spent the entire session on a tangent about how I'm allowing my past to dictate me... and our relationship... He wouldn't let me get a word in. It almost felt like I was having it out with my dad. God knows if I wanted to deal with that, I would have never run away from home at seventeen."

Ryland dropped her head, unsure how to respond. It wasn't the first time Charlie was like this, but it was rare. It took a lot to knock Charlie down. But when he was broken, it gutted Ryland. *How did this become a nightmare?* she thought. Another part of her wondered if maybe what they were both experiencing was merely growing pains.

Charlie leaned back and lifted his head, his lashes fluttering as he rapidly blinked. He sucked in a breath, fighting back whatever he was feeling. He stayed that way for a while. Ryland almost slipped away, partially to give him privacy. But, mostly, guilt was eating her conscience the more she was around Charlie. Yet, his hand found hers. Her heart flitted at his touch, drawing her back to him and pulling her away from the noise in her mind. With his russet brown sights on her, he said, "Meet me by the lake tonight. I'll set up dinner for us."

Ryland arched a brow at him. "Dinner?" she repeated, reminding him where they were and what was actually accessible.

But Charlie flashed a fleeting look, quickly erasing his sadness into oblivion as if it had never existed. "Jared and Xavier have got it all covered," he assured her.

Those old butterflies found their way back inside her. Soon, excitement seeped in as she pictured the two of them surrounded by serendipity, as they found themselves heart to heart again.

"All you need is a touch-up!" suggested Tathia. She skipped to the other side of the room Cheyenne shared with Xavier, where a straightener rested on a nightstand. She grabbed it, along with other hair moisturizers, before returning to Ryland's side. The redhead was seated patiently in the chair her friends had set her in, though it felt odd being the center of attention.

As Tathia rested her chosen materials and tools, she added, "Let's straighten out those curls, give you some layers, then turn your hairdo into a balayage blowout."

Cheyenne and Sabrina squealed at the opportunity of witnessing a makeover.

"You *definitely* should do it!" Sabrina urged the scarlet rose. "You'll knock the lights out of Charlie. He'll never see it coming."

Cheyenne leaped to her feet, abandoning her seat on the floor where she'd been sharing a box of cereal with Sabrina. She headed straight for the closet, a determined glint in her eyes. After shuffling through clothes for a few moments, she fished out what she was looking for—a soft lavender dress with a deep cowl bodice and spaghetti straps. The skirt seemed a bit short for Ryland's height compared to Cheyenne's 5'4" stature, but after convincing Ryland to ditch her usual boho chic ensemble, the dress hung just above her knees.

Cheyenne allowed Ryland to keep the silver chandelier earrings, since all the friends agreed that they complemented the dress. She did, however, ditch the many rings on her hands, except for the marquise diamond she held so dear. Then, Tathia went to work on Ryland's fiery ringlets.

After about thirty minutes, Tathia's promise of a makeover was realized. She held up a mirror, letting Ryland evaluate the final result. Her jaw dropped at her. "Wow!" the redhead let out. Then, Ryland peered up at the beaming faces around her, gratitude welling up in her eyes.

"Don't you let that tear drop!" Sabrina chided. "You'll ruin your makeup."

Cheyenne flew to the rescue, fanning the scarlet rose with a fashion magazine. A chuckle escaped Ryland. She was right—there wasn't time to get emotional. She had to meet Charlie. After pulling her friends into one last hug, Ryland went on her way.

As she walked toward their cabin, her heart tugged at her legs. A part of her was excited to finally spend some time with Charlie, but this was overshadowed by the weight of Sherrie's words. Sure, some of the things Sherrie brought up seemed to make sense, but Ryland couldn't shake off her advice. *Find something outside of Charlie?* As far Ryland was concerned, everything she's done up to this point was driven by her own desire for a stable mind.

Soon enough, Ryland found Charlie behind their cabin, sitting a few feet away from the lake. She stopped short in her tracks, a gasp pouring from her lips. Candlelights were scattered everywhere, resembling tiny fairies dancing around the picnic he had set up. A beautiful beige blanket was laid out, held down by a basket filled with all sorts of goodies—wrapped sandwiches, fruits, and a bottle of virgin spritz. As a cherry on top, there were desert lilies sprinkled as decoration. That was so like Charlie to remember her favorite flower.

She hadn't realized how long she'd been standing there until Charlie was already gliding toward her. He, too, seemed taken back by the sights of her. As Ryland drank him in, her heart grieved with a heavy conscience. His height was accentuated by solid black jeans, complemented by a matching leather jacket and a tucked-in linen shirt, which was unbuttoned at the top. That cross necklace was perfectly placed on his chest, glimmering like the moon above. His luminous mane appeared longer as it had been brushed out into loose waves. Although his hair was slightly damp.

Now standing face to face and lost for words, it took a moment to gather themselves. But Charlie broke the silence. "Call it a honeymoon phase, I don't care..." he murmured, his fingers entangling themselves in her hair. *"I miss you."*

With his necklace in her hand, she lifted her gaze at him. If only he knew how much she longed for him.

Charlie led her to the spot he picked out for them, distributing their plates and pouring their drinks. As she watched him, Ryland was captivated by the symphony of wildlife synchronizing in the background. The low, full-bodied hum of cicadas, crickets, and the hoots of owls, along with the pitched chorus of croaking frogs surrounding the lake, created a mesmerizing melody. However, it was Charlie's voice, gentle and low, that stole the show.

"Now that it's *just* us," he began, "I want you and I to lay everything out on the table."

That's when her stomach dropped. Ryland lowered her head, her mind gnawing at her again. She couldn't ignore things any longer, either. "Yeah, um... I'm starting to think you might have been right from the beginning."

She felt his hand slip under hers.

"Lately, I feel like we can't seem to reconnect and stay that way," he said. Ryland casted her brown globes on him, confusion clouding her gaze. "I miss nights like this, with you and I talking things out. I feel like even last weekend was barely a taste of what we used to be."

Ryland averted her eyes, trying to hide the ache that whelmed in her chest. But Charlie didn't know that.

"We're almost two weeks in," he continued. Then, he reached out to her, his warmth caressing her. "*How* is this place helping us?"

She clung to silence as retrospection brought conviction, both in epiphanies and protests. One voice, however, was louder than the rest. "It takes two to make this work," she finally said, turning to Charlie. "Last I remember, you're the one who has been more distant."

Charlie leaned back, his eyes wide with shock. "Ryland, I've been trying to give you space."

"*And you're mad at me for that?*" she shot back.

"No!" he defended. "I'm worried about you, and you won't *talk* to me. Don't you think I know you too well not to notice?"

The fiery belle straightened up, narrowing her gaze. "If you know me so well, then you *should know* what's bothering me."

The quiet storm beside her had finally brewed, burying his face in his hands. All Ryland could do was wait for him to say *anything,* fearing she might have pushed him too far. When he finally recovered, Charlie looked at her—really looked at her. In the dimness of the night, she saw the full weight of her words in his glazed eyes.

"Ryland," he began, his tone grave, "don't you find it strange that we haven't had a single session together. I mean a real one for a couple, not us in a room with a bunch of miserable people."

That struck a chord within her. How could she refute? It was strange. Still, she tried to reason, "Maybe Sherrie thinks it's best if we focus on ourselves before we do that," she explained. "She *is* treating us like a special case, remember?"

Charlie just blinked at her, like she spoke a different language. Then he turned away, shaking his head. "She never explained what that meant."

Ryland's gaze sharpened as frustration simmered beneath the surface. "Did she have to?" she snapped. "I'm not the only one with things to figure out, Charlie. Sometimes... even *you are* a mystery to me."

Just like that, her words struck like a blow. His head whipped in her direction, his brows knitted, yet his stare was delicate on her. "How am I a mystery to you?"

The fiery belle licked her teeth, torn with herself. She had gone a step too far. Still, she went on.. "Is it possible that Maxwell might have been right? What if you are holding yourself back?"

That earned a scoff from her fiancé, but it didn't seem he meant to.

Ryland let out a sigh, still aiming to break through to him. "I know this has a lot to do with Lydia—"

"Don't!" Charlie cut her off, his eyes brimming with fury and heartache. *"Don't you dare."*

The way his voice throbbed tormented her in the worst way. She squeezed her eyes closed, knowing that her next words had to be said. "You can't control everything. Maybe you *are* letting your pain dictate you ...and our relationship..."

Just like that, his eyes flared with horror. Ryland quickly realized what she had just done to him. It was what she feared.

"So, you agree with Maxwell?" he pressed, though the infliction in his voice sounded like he knew the answer all along. As soon as he said this, breaths hitched in their throats. He combed back his hair, blinking back the gloss thickening in his eyes.

Ryland tried to call out to him, but he pulled away.

"I need to go," he said, brushing her off.

Again, Ryland tried to stop him.

But he ignored her attempt. "Do you have your card?"

She searched his face, hoping for any sign of Charlie. But she did not find him. With her head hung, all she could do was reply with a nod. She watched limply as the dark-haired beau climbed to his feet, though he seemed still chained to Ryland. He glanced back at the scarlet rose, and for a second she hoped he'd come back to her. But he sucked in a breath like a long drag and walked away, leaving her with a heart knocked to pieces.

CHAPTER EIGHTEEN

Charlie was already up and dressed by the time Ryland got out of bed. The clock on her night stand flashed: 9:30 AM. The sky was blanketed with gray clouds, which were swell and threatened to pour out what built up in them. The dark-haired beau sat on their emerald-colored couch with his head hanging low and hands buried deep in his hair. Ryland quickly slipped on some clothes and met Charlie where he was. He lifted his eyes, snidely landing on what she wore. "I wish you'd stop wearing that," he scoffed.

Just like that, they were back to snapping at each other. "I wish you'd start wearing it," she retaliated.

The young couple was still raw from last night. It cut her deep that Charlie seemed to have stopped trying. She lowered herself next to him, attempting to reach out again. Instead of that warmth she longed for, he stiffened. Her throat tightened as a lump swelled inside. "Please talk to me," she begged him.

But he pulled himself away, heading straight for the door. She raised her voice again, probing him. Finally, he responded to her. "I'm going to Maxwell and Sherrie," he simply stated.

Ryland's eyes widened. "Don't!" But he was already out the door. So she chased after him. "Charlie!"

He kept walking.

Ryland finally caught up, though she had to endure the heavy silence between them. She had never known Charlie to be this way. Crudely, Sherrie's words crawled around her mind like spiders. Then, eerily and swiftly, Mama's voice swallowed her thoughts, screeching louder than her own. Ryland didn't hear the sigh escape her lips, nor did she notice that Charlie had finally looked back at her. He stopped them short in their tracks, leaving them in the middle of the dirt path—face to face, yet utterly alone. The sky darkened with each moment blurring by, and for a second, Ryland felt as though it was about to crash down on them. Charlie reached out, resting a hand on her cheek. Suddenly, he was wiping away tears she hadn't realized were there until then. The awareness of his brushing thumb and the salt-soaked frustration had her shaking.

"*Please* don't make us leave..." she pleaded.

Charlie squeezed his eyes closed but pressed his forehead against hers. "You are scaring me, dove," he said. It had been a while since he last called her that. Ryland almost didn't recognize it. "This isn't like you. *I don't care* what Sherrie, Maxwell, Breanna, Tyler, or anyone else in this hellbound place says. I know you, and *you know that.*"

"How are you so sure?" she fired back. "People are capable of changing. Even in ways that make you uncomfortable. You *can't* stop that."

"Not if you're changing for the worse."

Ryland folded her arms, glaring at him. "How am I changing for the worse?"

Instead of biting back, he locked his gaze on her with his hand remaining on her cheek. "The person I met six years ago was so self-assured and bright with life," he reminded her. Then he paused as his eyes shifted around her face. She almost felt them peeling away the depths of her. But sadness seeped into those intricate dark orbs as he searched. His shoulders dropped, eventually giving up.

That cut Ryland deep. If only he knew she'd been searching all this time.

The conversation died as Charlie kept moving forward. She let him lead the way, praying he wouldn't take her anywhere close to what she feared.

The rest of the way was spent in excruciating silence. He'd look her way but she would be far gone again in another thought. When she'd peek at him, his mind was elsewhere. Somehow, the couple picked up a path that was familiar to Ryland. The closer they approached the area it led to, Ryland quickly realized they were headed for the Turners' home. Her stomach twisted in knots. It felt like she was about to choke on her heart. As soon as they entered the pathway through their lawn, her footsteps levied as they closed the gap between them and the porch steps. She almost tugged on Charlie's hand but she dreaded another spat between them. Before she knew, the young couple stood at the top of the porch steps. Ryland attempted one more protest, but it clung to her lips as no sound came out.

Sucking in a breath, Charlie lifted an arm and rammed his knuckles against the door. But no response. Just silence. So, he knocked again, but to no avail.

Charlie finally turned away when the door flew open. Standing at the door was Maxwell. As he and the dark-haired beau met each other's gaze, Ryland captured an uncanny look in Maxwell's eyes, almost like a scowl. Alarmed, she shifted her sights on Charlie. Was there something else going on than he's letting on? As quickly as it came, whatever she thought she saw had swiftly been smothered by forged kindness and surprise. Especially as soon as Maxwell spotted the scarlet rose standing beside Charlie.

"Oh, hi!" he greeted the couple. "What can I do for you two?"

Ryland peered up, silently begging why they were at his front door.

"I'd like for my fiancée and I to have a session together," Charlie petitioned. "Since we've been here, we haven't had one."

His bluntness struck like a sharp blow because Maxwell seemed to have lost his composure. But only for a moment. Ryland's eyed Charlie, hoping he'd sense her plea not to ruin things for them. But her perfect storm remained unmoved until he got an answer.

The Turner widened his smile, though the same strange look from moments ago resurfaced. "What would make you think that?" he tested Charlie.

Charlie arched a brow at him. "I may not know much about the trade, but I think many counselors with just as much experience would share the same concern." That was enough to knock the smile off Maxwell's face.

The aging blonde paused for a moment, scanning his every move. Ryland tugged at Charlie's hand, still desperately grabbing his attention. But Maxwell responded, "We can set something up today. How does four o'clock sound?"

"Splendid." And that was that. Satisfied, Charlie turned his back and headed down the stairs. Ryland felt the urge to mouth "I'm sorry" to Maxwell, who gave her an assuring nod.

Ryland once again found herself having to catch up to Charlie. This time, she didn't stop when she reached his side. Instead, she planted herself in his tracks, forcing him to halt. "What was that all about!" she demanded.

Charlie blinked at her, but Ryland didn't budge. He heaved out a sigh, a mystifying look branching across his face. "I know this sounds weird..." he began, "but I feel like those two are trying to split us up."

Even Ryland had to pause for a moment, those words struggling to filter through her. "That's literally unethical!" she refuted. Still, such a thought struck a chord inside in a way she couldn't face.

"Think about it," Charlie pleaded.

Ryland shook her head, trying to rid his words from her mind. For as long as she knew the Turners, they had been so kind to the couple. She finally found a place where she could peel off the weight of her past. But was it truly just a mirage in the desert?

The hours dragged as the couple waited intently for four o'clock to strike. Ryland, especially, grew more antsy as the clock slowly ticked.

Finally, in came the appointed time, as a knock echoed against the walls. The pair stiffened as Ryland's insides diminished like a growing black hole. Charlie opened the door, revealing the typical beaming faces they expected all along. "Hi!" Sherrie beamed. "We thought it'd be great to meet you here. The familiarity of your space should help ease things a bit."

Charlie didn't seem to mind. In fact, he eagerly stepped aside and let them in. Although, as the Turners bypassed him, their stare lingered on his deep blue linen buttoned shirt and washed out denim jeans.

The older couple and the dark-haired beau moved to the parlor room, where Ryland had been waiting. Sherrie and Maxwell grabbed two wooden chairs from the kitchen area, allowing Ryland and Charlie to take the couch. Despite the cushioned relief, Ryland felt as if she might sink to the floor under the tempered pressure between them. She sat on the edge, her knees pressed tightly together, fingers clenched around her wrist. Sherrie and Maxwell were positioned across from her, their practiced smiles soft and reassuring. Charlie was beside her, but the space between them might as well have been miles. Yet, with his shoulder resting against hers, she still had a grip on reality.

Maxwell cleared his throat and opened a brown saddle-stitched notebook, scanning its contents briefly before raising his eyes to meet Charlie's. "I want to start today by acknowledging how brave it is for you both to be here, especially with everything that's been happening between you two."

Ryland nodded mechanically, though her gaze remained fixed on the woven patterns of the wooden floors.

"I agree," Sherrie chimed in softly. "It takes a lot of courage to be vulnerable in this way. Relationships aren't easy. And Charlie, I know you've been feeling disconnected from Ryland lately. That's understandable, especially when one partner is undergoing a lot of changes. That tends to happen with personal growth."

Charlie shifted uncomfortably. "I am worried about her growth but in a different way. I just—"

Maxwell cut him off with a raised hand and a patronizing smile. "Of course. No need to explain yourself," he said. "We're here to help *both* of you, but sometimes growth in one person can trigger insecurities in the other."

Ryland glanced at Charlie, who blinked back at the aging blond, completely lost for words. *Insecurity?* Ryland repeated in her mind. Was that what he was feeling? Was he truly scared, or was she pushing him away all this time?

It seemed that Charlie regained his composure, but his eyes darkened. Yet his voice remained calm. Dead calm. "It's not *insecure* to worry about the wellbeing of my partner, especially with what I know she's been through—both of us have so much to heal from," he said. "I don't want anyone or anything to stop her from what she needs. But I don't think all of this—" he gestured around the room "—has been helping her, or us."

Sherrie smiled sweetly, but there was something icy thickening beneath it. "It's not about blame, Charlie. We all have our limitations. Sometimes the people we love, unknowingly, can hinder us because they fear losing who we used to be." Without giving Charlie a chance to respond, she turned to Ryland, her voice tender and inviting. "How have you been feeling? Do you ever think Charlie holds you back at times?"

Ryland quickly lifted her head as a wave of shock rattled her bones like lightning. Her heart pounded so loudly that she almost didn't hear the question. The ranch had offered her so much—a chance to bury the pain, an escape from the daily hauntings. But there was a small voice inside her, growing louder each day. It was terrifying because it echoed the worries in Charlie's mind. If she gave it even an inch of her attention, she feared that everything might fall apart. She glanced at Charlie, whom she loved to the last drop, but the weight of the Turners' words pressed down on her.

"I don't know..." Ryland's voice was barely above a whisper. "I know... I feel stuck."

Charlie looked back at her, as if silently pleading her to open up.

Maxwell nodded sympathetically, as if he had anticipated her response all along. "That's completely normal, Ryland. It's a sign of growth, and sometimes growth means shedding old relationships, or at least stepping back from them to see if they're truly serving us."

Charlie's eyes flew at him with his jaw clenched. "That's not what this is about," he insisted, his voice growing firmer. "Don't you hear it in her voice? That's not the person I knew *before we came here*. It hurts to see her like this, and none of you are helping as much as you think."

Sherrie leaned forward, her eyes narrowing ever so slightly, but her tone remained slick and velvety like honey. "Charlie, I know this might feel threatening to you, but we're simply observing patterns. She's on the right path. As for you... you've been so... *resistant*."

"How?" Charlie shot back, his voice sharpening with frustration.

Maxwell butted in. "You're not taking heed to any of our efforts," he explained. "We thought Tyler was the right person for you because, hey, you're not the only case with a similar reaction. If you want to be that safe space for Ryland as you claim to be, you have to let go of all those pent up emotions and control. Ryland's been open with us about her childhood. It helps to go back and see what exactly triggered our perception of life. We still don't know much about you. I don't think Ryland does either."

Charlie shook his head, dismissing Maxwell's words. "No, that's not true," he refuted, but his tone never raised.

"As for my childhood, I let all of it go a long time ago. Yes, I wish I knew my real parents. Yes, I miss my sister. But those things have nothing to do with my marriage to Ryland. I acknowledge that for someone, a past like mine might have a part to play. But I can't force myself to play the role of a headcase if I'm simply *not*."

Ryland's heart twisted at the word "marriage." How did she forget so quickly? Their wedding day was approaching fast and it killed her inside that she and Charlie were so far from each other. She almost broke down at how Charlie spoke about it with such hope.

But Sherrie's voice cut through her thoughts like a scalpel. "Sometimes, though, a marriage can hinder a person's true calling." Her gaze flickered between them. "You've both come so far individually, but we've noticed that whenever we touch on Ryland's potential, Charlie, you seem... uneasy."

Charlie let out a laugh so bitter and so distant, that even Ryland recoiled under the sound of his voice. "I'm not uneasy," he said, flatly. "Ryland had been someone who reached for the stars. I watched her fight her way out of the darkest places. I was there when she needed just one person in her corner. You don't know those nights but I do. That's why I *know* this place is killing her. You two are not helping us. You are trying to tear us apart."

Maxwell's eyes darkened, but his voice remained calm. "Charlie, you're the one who asked us for this session," he pointed out. "And we've only ever wanted what's best for Ryland—and for you. But not everyone is ready for the level of transformation we offer here. It takes humility. And sometimes, when one partner resists, it can stop the other from fully blooming."

But Charlie wasn't swayed. "I asked for this session to confront you in front of *her*." He looked back at the scarlet rose evidently wilting beside him. "I need her to see who's on her side. I need her to know that she's not going crazy. Everything she's feeling is okay, but all she has to do is remember that she always had someone with her."

But it was all too much for Ryland. She felt as if she were being pulled in two opposing directions. She didn't want to believe Charlie was right—that the Turners were trying to destroy their marriage. But Maxwell's words and Sherrie's gentleness offered a sense of calm to the storm inside her—a way to stay at the ranch and hold onto the fragile peace she'd found.

Charlie wasn't done yet. "And this isn't about blooming—it's about control." His eyes locked onto Maxwell's. "I'm not going to sit here and let you do that to her."

For the first time, the mask on Maxwell's face slipped. His smile was gone, replaced by something colder, harder. "Charlie, maybe you're the one who's controlling her. Have you considered that? Maybe Ryland would be better off without the weight you put on her."

The words sliced through the air like a blade, and Ryland's breath caught in her throat. She looked at Charlie, seeing the hurt flash in his eyes. Was Maxwell right? Was Charlie afraid of losing her if she truly embraced this new life? Or... was Charlie right?

Silence settled between them like a thick fog, oppressive and heavy. Ryland glanced between the two men, the weight of the decision pressing down on her. Finally, Maxwell folded his notebook as he and Sherrie rose to their feet. As they walked past the couch to get to the door, Sherrie rested a hand on Ryland's shoulder, her emerald eyes looking intently into Ryland's troubled gaze. "You know you have a safe space with us," she assured.

With that, the Turners left the cabin, leaving their words to marinate between the couple. Charlie got up and headed for the bathroom, closing the door behind him. Still, Ryland could hear the faint sound of weeping spilling through the walls.

CHAPTER NINETEEN

Charlie spent a while in the bathroom, and all Ryland could do was sit on the couch, waiting for him. But as the seconds passed, the guilt that had festered for days in the scarlet rose finally morphed into a monster of its own, plaguing her already wilting petals. She pulled her knees to her chest and hid her face in her palms, fighting back a set of thoughts seeping into the walls of her mind. *Maybe we should take a break...* her mind whispered. Though it horrified her, she found herself gradually agreeing. *Maybe Sherrie was right. Maybe she had to focus on*

herself for now. Maybe Mama had known all along that she could not handle marriage—not in this state.

"I should have listened..." spilled out of Ryland's lips.

"What?"

Her heart hitched in her throat. She hadn't heard the bathroom door open, nor Charlie's footsteps in the room. She finally got a look at him—a real good look at him. His stare was tender and glossed with worry. But his jaw was clenched, and his shoulders straightened. She tried to reach out to him. "Charlie—"

"You should've listened to Sherrie and Maxwell?"

She levied a sigh as her fingers flew to her hair and tugged at the roots. "That's not what I meant!" she defended. But as quickly as she did, Ryland fell through her own defense. "I mean..."

Charlie lowered himself next to her, his eyes widened and face now soft. "Ryland, what is going on with you?" he pleaded.

But that struck a nerve. Ryland shot to her feet and walked away from the couch. She didn't get far before Charlie reached out for her hand, but she swatted him away. "How is it that you are the only one who doesn't see what's wrong with me!" she barked.

Charlie froze in his tracks, clearly appalled by what he was hearing. "Ryland, there is nothing wrong with you," he fought back, but his voice never raised once at her.

Her tone sharpened and its volume heightened. "Yes! Yes, there is!" she said, matter-of-factly. "I can't be a wife. I can't be a mother. I can't even be good to myself. My head keeps screaming at me and I can't get it to stop!"

Charlie's hands raised to his face, his fingertips pinching his nose, trying his best to hold back the tears that threatened to fall. But they were already rolling down his cheeks. He took a few moments to collect himself, and when he finally did, he lowered his hands and inched closer to her. "It's normal to be afraid, Ryland," he tried to soothe her. "You don't think I am? I'm terrified of a lot, but I don't let it consume me."

Ryland narrowed her eyes, though the disgust was directed at herself. "Not everyone is as strong as you," she countered. "I'm not strong. I never was."

Charlie shook his head, refusing to accept her words. "That doesn't mean you never will be."

At that, Ryland finally broke, as if someone had thrown a wrench at a wall of glass. "I can't..." she cried. Charlie tried to embrace her once again, but she pushed him away. "Not with you."

Both fell silent, unsure of where to steer the conversation. But Ryland couldn't calm down. She couldn't block out the voices echoing in her mind. Instead, she felt herself slowly succumbing to them. Almost miraculously, Charlie broke the silence, offering her a glimmer of relief. "Did I do something to hurt you?" he asked gently.

The sincerity in his voice stung. She squeezed her eyes shut, shaking her head. "You didn't do anything wrong..."

A look of defeat started to surface on his face. "I don't understand," Charlie expressed. "You didn't get this way overnight."

And just like that, the rage flooded back inside, as Ryland flashed her eyes at him. "Have you seriously not considered that maybe I've been this way all my life?" Her voice raised again, and her muscles tightened with frustration.

"Ryland—"

"What part of *broken* are you not getting, Charlie?" she snapped. Then she raised a hand in the direction of the door, as if the Turners were still there. "Sherrie and Maxwell see it. My mom sees it. My sister sees it, but God bless her because she doesn't have the heart to tell me. I'm sure all of our friends see it, both back home and here." Then she paused, trying to catch her breath to suppress the fury kindling hot inside her. It wasn't directed at him—just twenty years of pent-up emotions finally erupting. Though she tried her best to keep them from touching Charlie, she wondered why he kept fighting the obvious.

Charlie finally stepped back, letting her words sink in. After some time, the two just stood there with Ryland carefully analyzing every muscle and twitch. Charlie poised himself and challenged her with his next thought. "What you're saying about yourself is not true."

Ryland groaned.

"I've tried," she pleaded. "I wanted so hard to believe that I could be those things I want, but I simply can't. I can't love you when I don't love myself! I need to love myself first! Why are you trying so hard to keep me? Just leave me here!" With that, she spun on her heels, heading for their bedroom. Charlie didn't utter another word as he watched her pack the only two duffel bags he had. He didn't protest, call her name, or even flinch at the tears rolling down her cheeks. When all of his things were out of sight, Ryland walked up to him and handed him his bags. But he did not accept them. Ryland moaned, begging him to go. "Just leave me here. I need to get better."

Charlie placed his hand over hers, gently lowering them until she finally let his bags drop at their feet. This time, Ryland didn't resist as he wrapped his arms around her. They just stood there, her tears soaking into his shirt, but he didn't seem to mind. "You don't think I'm broken in many ways, too?" he said, his voice finally cutting through the noise in her mind. "I've walked through life with the fear of repeating what my parents did to my sister. Liya and I struggled with our identities. We didn't know our real parents, and our substitutes weren't any more nurturing. Even with all that money and those lavish trips, it felt like they were just stuffing our mouths with gold to look like prized parents in everyone else's eyes. Liya suffered inside her whole life. So, because of their neglect, she ran away. Because of their neglect, I ran away. Liya and I were so focused on our own pain that we ended up tearing apart the only family we had—each other. Now, I live in regret, learning life's greatest lesson the hard way."

Ryland leaned away, just enough to peer up at him. She allowed herself to become immersed in his eyes, which held her so dearly. For the first time in a long time, she felt the serendipity she'd been searching for.

"Love is supposed to be a balanced flow between people," Charlie continued. "It's not about one person consuming and only giving under certain conditions. It's those kinds of people who burn bridges, devour their communities, and isolate themselves on their own islands. Everyone wants to be loved, but many people actually want their egos to be worshiped. So, they consume love like a black hole. And what happens when everyone becomes like that? There won't be enough love—if any at all—left for anyone, not even for the people who only care about being loved."

Ryland felt a bit lost, but at the same time, his words started to make sense. She just needed to understand why. "What are you saying?" she asked, willing to finally let him in.

Charlie tilted his head, admiring the woman gazing back at him. "I'm saying you're right," he told her. Ryland blinked, her heart nearly hitting the ground. But then he added, "I've had many reasons to leave. We've weathered storms over the years, but I've watched them bloom into something beautiful between us. I'm scared to be a dad, but I refuse to let my loveless childhood stop me from being a present and faithful father to our children. So, if that's possible for me, I know our kids will have a loving mother. You have to believe that for yourself."

At that moment, Ryland finally let go. With her eyes closed and her head bowed, she gathered up her past, her pain, and the haunting voices in her mind—and deliberately, delicately, set them free. Strength began to stir within her, enough to stand on her own two feet. But as she lifted her gaze to meet Charlie's, she knew that the fragile bud of resilience growing inside her would need tending. It would take time, and his steady presence, to help that strength weave its way through the tangled roots of old wounds that had held her captive for so long. With that thought alone, a chuckle escaped her, though tears brimmed her eyes. "Why didn't I tell you this in the first place?" she said, chiding herself. "I feel like I wasted time we could have spent together."

"It was never a waste," Charlie murmured, dismissing the very thought.

Ryland shot him a teasing look. "You hated it here."

He let out a chuckle, unable to deny it. She watched as he scratched his head, a spark of mischief lighting up his eyes. "I hated what this place was doing to you," he admitted. "But—the Turners and our counselors aside—it's not so bad. I'll give it this much: the scenery is beautiful."

Ryland's gaze softened as his words sparked a thought that lingered in her mind. "So... should we stay?"

Charlie glanced down at his packed bags, then back at her. "More like, do you want to stay?" he teased, stirring another laugh inside Ryland, like medicine to her heart.

Her eyes flicked to her side of the room, then back to him. "Honestly..." she began, "is it okay if you give me some time to think about it?"

He gently cradled her face, his hands warm against her cheeks, as he leaned in and pressed a tender kiss to her temple. A flutter of butterflies stirred in her belly, filling her with a warmth that felt like home. When he pulled back, his eyes lingered on her, soft and steady. "Take all the time you need," he murmured. "Just let me know when you're ready."

She could always count on him.

CHAPTER TWENTY

The couple ditched their sessions for the day to spend it together. They snuck off the ranch on their own, carefree in broad daylight. Ryland was driven by a sudden craving for diner food and milkshakes, and luckily, they found a spot about fifteen minutes away. Once satisfied with a meal that didn't come from the Common Hall, they wandered next door into a vinyl shop. They thumbed through the various collections, each album and artist sparking conversations of nostalgia. This time, neither Charlie nor Ryland felt distant from those memories;

instead, they relished the reminiscing. They even bought a Bryan Adams record as a souvenir to mark the day.

By the time they found the will to head back to the ranch, they were exhausted—but in the best way. It was exactly how Ryland wanted it to be. That night, she rested her mind, though she soon slipped into another state entirely.

The fiery belle found herself in a very familiar place, but it was neither of the homes she grew up in. Yet, she was back in Flagstaff. She recognized the floor panels in the hallway of her old apartment building. She sensed she was already on the third floor, where her apartment was at the very end of the hall. So, she made her way there until she stood before the door, staring at the numbers plated above: 310. Instinctively, she reached into the pocket of her white denim skirt and pulled out a key.

As she stepped inside, her eyes immediately caught sight of a figure hovering by the living room window. She froze, fear seizing her from moving a single muscle. Once her vision finally adjusted, the figure's identity became clear. The woman's long, deep-brown tresses were pulled into a mid-rise ponytail, swinging softly as she turned her head, peering through the window. Ryland recognized the typical turtleneck style paired with wide-legged slacks and expensive pumps. As sunlight streamed across her face, the woman's lashes and the color of her irises captured a bronze hue in the light, reflecting off the bangle that slid down her arm as she tucked a hand under her chin.

"Mama?" Ryland called out.

The woman whipped around at the sound of her daughter's voice. For a moment, her face was devoid of thought or emotion. Then, in a flash, it was overtaken by a look Ryland had long grown accustomed to. This time, however, Ryland didn't cower. Instead, a smile tugged at her lips, soothing her heart like an emollient for her gradually healing wounds.

Ryland's eyes fluttered open, the ceiling above coming into focus. The soft snores from Charlie's side of the bed tickled her ears, drawing her attention in his direction. He didn't see the appreciation plastered on her face as she reached out, brushing away a few stray strands that had tangled in his lashes. Then, she slipped out of bed.

She didn't have a clear goal in mind, but she was drawn to the couch and compelled to her phone in hand. Unlocking the screen, her thumb lingered over Mama's number. With her lower lip tucked between her teeth, Ryland hesitated. Part of her still dreaded any interaction with Mama, but another part held onto the bit of courage she still had from earlier. So, she lifted the phone to her ear.

She listened as the line rang a few times, the final ring signaling it was about to go to voicemail. Her arm started to lower, thinking this might have been a blessing in disguise. Just as she was about to hang up, a voice broke through on the other end.

"Hello?" It was Mama, her voice sending chills through Ryland.

The scarlet rose sucked in a breath, attempting to smother any ounce of fear left in her. "Hey... it's me."

"Ryland!" Mama yelped. "Why—" Even from the other end, she could hear her mother choke up. Guilt washed over Ryland, but it didn't chain itself to her. Not like those many times before. Instead, it was merely a heart of penitence. "I haven't heard from you in *weeks*!

Callie told me you were at a rehabilitation center with Charlie. *What is going on?* Are you okay?"

Ryland's eyes widened. To hear such earnesty laced in Mama's voice was so foreign, yet so stirring. She was lost for words. "Um, we're okay…" she assured.

"Why?" Mama pried, though her tone was like mirth. Ryland marveled at this. By now, they'd be knee-deep in another heated spat. "Please tell me what's going on? What kind of center is this?"

"Mama, I'm at a ranch," the scarlet rose explained. "It's a retreat for couples. I'm not locked up in a ward or anything."

A deep sigh poured through the speakers, but it wasn't cynical. "I'm just glad to hear from you."

Those words stung Ryland's eyes. Before she knew it, she lost her composure. Mama called out to her, but Ryland couldn't respond, too stifled to lift her voice. Mama waited patiently as her daughter sobbed. Whether it had been realized or not that a prayer was answered, it was a long-awaited breakthrough between them. Finally, Ryland gathered herself, drinking in a few breaths to freshen her voice. As soon as she regained the strength to speak, the scarlet rose opened up.

"I called to set some things straight with you," she told her mother. "There's so much I want to say, but I realize now that I'd sound like a broken record. This weight I've carried all these years, I just want to let it go. So, um, I'm saying... *I forgive you.*"

Silence fell between them as the moment lingered. Abruptly, sniffles broke through from the other end. Ryland pressed the phone harder to her ear and squeezed her closed eyes tighter, anticipating anything at this point. Finally, Mama returned, her voice so rendering and emotions raw. "You have no idea how much I needed to hear that," she said. "Something brought me to my knees these past days. It was after I heard about you from Callie. All I could think about were the two little girls I—and your father—have failed. I prayed so hard that neither of you would leave my life."

Those words wrecked Ryland, but she couldn't help to listen to each one that spilled forth from her mother's heart.

"Now, here you are," Mama continued, "forgiving me before I could ask. How is that even possible?"

A smile formed on Ryland's face, as she wished for Mama to see the fondness in her eyes. "It was always possible..." she soothed. "I'm willing for us to start over."

That sparked a hearted laugh from Mama. "I'd love that!"

By the end of the call, Ryland was astonished. In such a short time, she witnessed the restoration of two relationships she once thought were lost. For so long, it felt like wishful thinking—a prayer she believed missed Heaven's ears. But here she was, basking in the love of both Charlie and her mother.

CHAPTER TWENTY-ONE

As Ryland and Charlie stepped outside their cabin the next morning, on the agreement that they'd finish out the last few days of the program, her eyes drifted from him to their front door. Her eyes widened as she reached out to grab Charlie, quickly catching his attention and redirecting it to the door. It didn't take long for him to spot it—a red string taped to the wooden surface. His eyes hardened as he tore it from the door, holding it up with a scowl.

"I'm getting to the bottom of this today!" he declared, turning to Ryland.

She nodded, right behind him, though she wasn't entirely sure how he planned to do that. Still, she followed him up the hill, the Turner house quickly coming into view. As soon as they reached the top of the porch steps, Charlie knocked firmly on the door. He rammed his knuckles a few more times, refusing to take silence for an answer.

While he waited, Ryland stepped back, deciding to look around for herself. She wasn't sure what waited for her, but she felt a strange, unshakable hope that she'd run into one of the Turners—or maybe Sabrina. She maneuvered around the house, heading toward the back. As expected, no one was on the property except herself, Charlie, and a couple of horses grazing freely nearby. So, she circled back to join her fiancé.

He lifted his arms in exasperation as she approached. "Did you find anything?"

She shook her head. "Not a single clue." She combed her fingers through her hair, a shiver of anxiety prickling her skin. "This is really scaring me. Should we call the police?"

Charlie opened his mouth but before he could utter a word, another voice chimed in.

"What do you need the police for?"

The couple whipped their heads in the direction of the voice to find Maxwell climbing the porch steps toward them. His face was twisted with narrowed eyes and brows furrowed. But Ryland stepped forward, grabbing the red string from Charlie's hand and dangling it in front of Maxwell. He didn't flinch nor showed the slightest bit of surprise. Still, she pressed on, saying, "I'm starting to think someone has been stalking us."

Maxwell raised both hands, as if trying to calm a spooked horse. "Let's slow down before we bring in Uncle Sam, alright?"

Ryland's brows knitted, taken aback by his dismissiveness. Fortunately, Charlie stepped in. "We're talking about our safety," he pointed out. "We've been seeing these things since before we even came here."

"So, why are you knocking on my door?" Maxwell asked, defensively. "You think we have something to do with that? Mighty bold of you, jumping to conclusions..."

The couple exchanged a look, both unsure how this conversation had escalated so quickly. "That's not what we're saying at all," Charlie replied, keeping his tone even. "We just thought we'd warn you. The same person harassing us might be targeting others on the ranch."

Maxwell's demeanor shifted in an instant. A smile streamed across his face, an attempt to soften the tension, but Ryland still sensed an edge of contempt. "Let's dial it back, okay?" he said in a low, steady tone. "How about you hand me that, and I'll have a few staff members check the area around your cabin. How does that sound?"

All the couple could do at that point was walk away, dejected and unsettled. They left Maxwell standing on the porch, his words hanging in the air around him. As they disappeared down the hill, Charlie rubbed soothing circles into Ryland's hand with his thumb. "We'll figure it out," he assured her.

But Ryland remained restless. She couldn't shake the way Maxwell had bristled. For the first time, she started to understand what Charlie had been trying to tell her. Just as they were far enough away from any potential eavesdroppers, Charlie stopped and turned to Ryland, his gaze locked in on her.

"Do you trust me?" he asked, his voice firm.

She blinked, startled by that question. "What? Of course, I do."

"Good," he said. "I'll need you to."

Ryland jerked back, examining every possible motive behind his words. "What are you talking about?"

"Maxwell has no right to tell us we can't go to the police," he said resolutely. "So, I'm going to find the nearest precinct to at least file a report."

Ryland's eyes widened. "I'm not letting you go alone!" she cried. "What if someone follows you? What if something happens while you're gone? What if I need you?"

"Have one of the girls stay with you," Charlie suggested calmly. "We also have the axe back at the cabin. If you need it, don't be afraid to use it."

She bit her lip, rolling around the idea in her mind, but it didn't ease her. She especially hoped things wouldn't escalate to the point of needing the axe. Still, she agreed to have one of their friends stay with her while Charlie was away. But anxiety started to gnaw at her. "What if Sherrie and Maxwell notice you're gone? What do I tell them if you don't get back in time?" she asked. "They already have us under a microscope since we missed half the day yesterday."

Charlie gently placed a hand under her chin, drawing her face closer to his until their noses nearly touched. "Please, trust me."

"But—"

"They already think I'm antisocial," he half-joked. "You can use that. I have no interest in salvaging my reputation in their eyes. They've tainted it enough."

Ryland opened her mouth to protest again. "Charlie, I don't like this."

But he stood firm. "Go," he insisted gently. "You're about to miss the morning group."

Before she could argue further, Charlie turned and walked away, heading in the direction of the Silverado. Ryland heaved a sigh, feeling both apprehensive and helpless, with no choice but to go along with his plan. She only hoped he knew what he was doing.

Ryland stepped inside the makeshift cottage, alone with a million new thoughts running through her mind. Cheyenne and Xavier's faces brightened at the sight of her, though Sherrie's emerald eyes were fixed on the scarlet beauty with laser intensity. Ryland tried to shake off the icy stare and focused on Cheyenne and Xavier, who embraced her as soon as she nestled beside them. Ryland could tell Cheyenne had so much to say, but, with Sherrie hawk-eyeing the group, her lavender-haired friend stayed quiet.

Sherrie took her usual place in her high chair, looking down on the group circled around her. Yet, her attention never left Ryland. "Looks like we're missing one more person," she commented. Then she directed a more pointed question at Ryland. "So, where is Charlie?"

All eyes flew to the scarlet rose, igniting a fresh swarm of butterflies in her gut. She swallowed hard, as the way Charlie comforted seeped into mind. Still, she managed to muster an answer. "Sometimes, he withdraws..." she stated, attempting a nonchalant shrug. "Today is one of those days for him."

Sherrie simply nodded with a noncommittal "Hmm." Then, she turned back to the group and began teaching as usual. Ryland spent the next hour zoning out, her thoughts constantly drifting to Charlie. She closed her eyes and lifted a silent prayer, hoping he was at least safe if he hadn't yet reached a precinct.

Before she knew it, the clock had sped up, and Sherrie released the group to their daily activities. Cheyenne's soft hand rested on Ryland's shoulder, drawing her attention. "Are you okay?" she asked, finally free to voice her concern. Xavier mirrored her worries, his face bearing the same burden as his wife.

Ryland bit her lip, sifting through her mind for the right words. Her gaze traveled to Sherrie, who lingered by the door, watching the trio with an expression as cold and unmoving as stone, her emerald stare burning a hole into Ryland. The scarlet rose took a sharp breath, steeling herself to face the inevitable. Turning back to her friends, she assured them she was okay, but then reconsidered, recalling Charlie's advice. "Will you and the others be free tonight?" she asked. She tried her best to keep her tone steady, though even she could hear it shaking.

Xavier and Cheyenne didn't hesitate. "Whatever you need, we're here," Xavier reassured, unknowingly lifting a bit of the weight from Ryland's shoulders.

She flashed an appreciative smile at her friends. "Thanks," she said, glancing back at Sherrie. "I don't want to hold you two back."

Neither uttered another word. Though they were reluctant to leave Ryland on her own, Xavier and Cheyenne shuffled to the door, with the lavender-haired companion constantly glancing over her shoulder. As soon as they were gone, Ryland rose to her feet, just as Sherrie walked up to her.

"This is the second day in a row that we haven't seen him," Sherrie noted.

Ryland caught the accusatory edge in Sherrie's voice. "I'm aware," she replied, trying to swallow the anxiety crawling under her skin. "He gets overwhelmed easily. I think this whole thing might be taking a toll on him."

Sherrie scoffed. "That's a poor excuse..."

Ryland's heart sank, her mind going into a frenzy. Did Sherrie know where Charlie was? Had Maxwell figured out what they were up to? But Sherrie continued,

"It happens all the time here. We've had couples with one partner responsive to our program, while the other rejects it. Charlie is starting to show clear signs of rejection."

Ryland felt stupefied. The truth had been staring at her all along. "How could you say that?" she countered. "Shouldn't a counselor know that it takes time to respond to treatment?"

Sherrie tilted her head, her brows twitching slightly at Ryland's retort. "He himself has had twenty-three unsuccessful sessions," she retorted. But as swift as those words slipped out, Sherrie's eyes softened. She placed a hand on Ryland's arm, like a mother consoling a naive child. "Honey, I tried to warn you. It's time to face facts."

"Face facts?" Ryland repeated.

"He's holding you back. If I were you, I'd let it go." As soon as Ryland's flared orbs daggered at her, Sherrie raised her hands in a placating gesture, as if waving a white flag. "I know, I know. I normally don't say things like this to couples. Trust me, I'd never cross this line. But, Ryland, I see so much in you. I'm afraid you won't ever get another chance to scratch the surface."

Astonished, tears pricked the corners of Ryland's eyes. Sherrie reached out and cooed, "It's okay. It hurts, at first. But trust me, you'll thank me in the end."

What Sherrie didn't see was the wellspring of rage bubbling up within the fiery belle. Without another word, Ryland pulled away from her grasp and stalked off.

CHAPTER TWENTY-TWO

Ryland sat on the couch, checking and rechecking her phone. She had yet to receive the text she was hoping for. She did get more emails surrounding wedding plans, though she ignored them. A sigh escaped her lips as she tossed her phone on the coffee table. It had been about two hours since the evening group session. It wasn't as intense as the morning one, though Sherrie surveyed her every move. By the end of the class, Xavier and Cheyenne had agreed to meet her at the cabin. They wanted to gather the others.

As she waited for anyone to return, Ryland had long ditched the flannel uniform for a rustic red minidress and her go-to black booties. She had also helped herself to Charlie's collection and slipped into another one of his favorite denim jackets, a dark gray one with fringes running down the arms. While planted on their couch in the middle of the parlor room, she hugged his jacket tighter around her.

Suddenly, a soft set of knocks broke through the pressured silence. She flew to the door, not heeding the possibility of who might actually be on the other side. As soon as it was yanked open, she was greeted by six beaming smiles. "Finally!" she exasperated, then hastily brought them inside.

Tathia glanced around, immediately enthralled by whatever her eyes landed on. "You and Charlie have the best cabin!" she complimented. To the others, she said, "We should hang out here more often."

Sabrina scrunched her nose at Cheyenne and Xavier. "Yeah, your cabin is a bit stuffy."

Xavier gasped, looking playfully offended. "I'll have you know our place is a haven!"

Cheyenne rolled her eyes, teasingly. "If that's what you call it…"

As the group of friends settled in, with Tathia and Cheyenne on either side of the scarlet rose on the couch, all sets of eyes landed on her, expectantly. "So, what's going on?" Cheyenne asked. When she'd first walked in, Ryland had noticed Cheyenne's eyes scanning the place specifically. Equipped with the opportunity, her lavender-haired friend added, "Where exactly is Charlie?"

Xavier leaned forward, a wave of alarm crashing over the group, especially Desmond. "Wait, what?" he pried. "Why would Charlie be gone?"

"I hadn't seen him in any of our carpentry or archery classes," Desmond added. "Not even at the Common—and the guy can eat!"

Ryland dropped her head, inhaling a new gust of tenacity despite the nerves firing off in her mind. Then she peered back up at the group, ready to give an answer. "To put it plainly," she started, "Charlie and I think someone has been following us. I mean, since we started our trip before coming here." Then she stood up from the couch and moved to the table in the kitchen, where the string they'd last seen taped to their door still lay. She picked it up and, turning back to the group, waved it in the air. "We keep seeing this. I know it sounds crazy, but we keep seeing these taped to our doors wherever we stay. I mean, these things have literally followed us from Holbrook."

Sabrina's eyes lit with shock. "So that's why you two flew out of there!" she exclaimed. "It was like watching a couple of bats out of a cave with the way you and Charlie drove off."

Ryland nodded as she recalled every moment. "That was the first encounter."

But Sabrina kept staring at the string, wheels churning behind her piercing green eyes. Ryland was drawn to the young Turner and her thoughts, but just as her own mind started to raise questions, Jared spoke up. "So..." he started, shifting in his seat as his deep brown eyes slightly drifted to the side, fixed on something whispering in his ear, "You're saying that whoever might be following you is *here...* on the ranch?"

Ryland nodded. "Charlie should have already been at the precinct," she explained. Then her fingers tugged at her loose crimson bun. "He *should* be back by now."

All six pairs of eyes exchanged glances as silence settled over the room. Sabrina had mentally drifted from the group, her focus locked onto the string in Ryland's hand. The scarlet rose stepped back toward the circle, half-tempted to question Sabrina, but Tathia spoke up, reaching out to her. "We'll stay with you," she assured softly.

The rest of the group affirmed with a nod. Sabrina, on the other hand, finally broke out of her trance. "I know where I've seen that string," she said, unprovoked.

Brows raised at her, but not Ryland, who listened intently. "What?" said Tathia, her voice tight with shock.

Sabrina nodded, adding, "It was that night my parents tried breaking us up. After I stormed out of the house, I went to check on Desmond at his cabin. When I had to go back home, that's when I saw *that thing* taped to his door."

"Okay, *this is getting creepy*," Cheyenne interrupted. "Where is Charlie with the police?"

"I wish I knew..." Ryland murmured.

Looking at Ryland, Xavier asked, "Did either of you tell Maxwell and Sherrie?"

The fiery belle shot him a cynical look. "They're both a dead end," the words slipped from her lips faster than she'd intended. She quickly glanced at Sabrina, an apologetic look in her eyes.

To her surprise, Sabrina turned to Xavier and said, "She's right. They didn't help me when I told them about the one on Desmond's door."

Tathia wrinkled her nose in disgust. "How could your parents ignore something like that?"

"I don't know," Sabrina replied, shaking her head. "But I do know they hate even the mention of getting the police involved. They always go on about avoiding lawsuits and how difficult it is to protect a self-owned business. You know... the typical spiel of self-made gurus." The way Sabrina spoke that last line left a bitter taste in the air, as if saying it had soured her own mouth.

Xavier and Cheyenne looked crestfallen, grappling with Sabrina's revelation about her parents. "I never knew them to be like that," Cheyenne murmured, a distant look clouding her gaze. "They always seemed so helpful and open to everyone. For crying out loud, they save marriages."

Ryland scoffed at the thought, unintentionally drawing curious stares from the group. But she held her ground, her eyes fixed on Cheyenne as she spoke. "They may have saved yours," she said, her voice sharp, "but for some reason, they've had their claws out for mine."

Sabrina leaned forward, her eyes steeled with determination. "They better not," she whispered, her voice low and chilling.

Desmond shared the same fierce resolve. "Not on my watch," he added, his tone equally unyielding.

Xavier swallowed, visibly unsettled. "Okay, this is getting beyond scary…"

Jared took a step forward, positioning himself directly in front of Ryland. "You're not telling us everything," he said flatly. "What's going on?"

Ryland rolled her eyes, feeling half-offended but deeply tangled in their words and her own thoughts. "I'm not entirely sure what's going on!" she defended. "All I know is that I'm scared, I don't know where my fiancé is, and I swear Sherrie and Maxwell have been trying to break us up this entire time!" Her confession spilled out all at once, unstoppable. The words kept pouring out. "Charlie was trying to tell me, and I'm mad at myself that it took this long to notice. I feel like I landed us in a seriously messed-up situation we can't get out of!"

Ryland plopped back onto the couch, settling between Cheyenne and Tathia. Both wrapped their arms around her, doing their best to soothe her troubled mind.

"Ryland, you might be biting off more than you can chew," Tathia began, "but you and Charlie have us. You also have to trust that Charlie is doing what he said he'd do."

"It's not that I don't trust him," Ryland countered. "I simply don't trust what may or may not happen."

But Tathia gazed at her with a knowing smile dancing on her glossed lips. "What's the point of faith if you only rely on what makes sense? You'll be surprised when you learn to trust, even if you can't see it yet."

And that stuck with Ryland. But her fears remained.

The hours on the clock dragged on as they waited for Charlie's return. By midnight, the group of friends had finally passed out. But Ryland stayed awake. As the others slept in their spots in the parlor room, her eyes were fixed on the front door, with the moon streaming in as her only source of light. Every now and then, her gaze shifted to her phone, which still rested on the coffee table. But not once in those hours of waiting did it light up or buzz. Her fingers found the hem of Charlie's jacket and clenched the fabric. She was determined to wait, even as the hours of the night gradually wound down.

It wasn't until four in the morning that shuffling sounds picked up from the other side of the front door. Ryland's heart quickened in her chest as she jerked upright. The sounds paused for a moment, leaving her in wonder. Was it a fluke? Then the noises started up again.

Another part of her considered a different, more frightening possibility—that it was something sinister.

She found herself caught in a cycle of excitement and fear, chained to the couch, afraid to make a single move.

As if on cue to answer her racing mind, a click from the door sent chills down her spine. Then the door swung open, revealing a shadowy figure standing at the threshold. It moved inside the cabin, and just as Ryland was about to spring into action, a voice stopped her short.

"Did I wake you?" It was Charlie.

Without warning, her sights were flooded with overhead lights. She raised her hands to her face, attempting to adjust to the sudden burst of brightness. Once her vision cleared, she turned back to the doorway. The front door was now shut and secured. Charlie lingered in the foyer, his eyes sweeping over the faces now awake and staring at him, along with Ryland.

"Now we're up," Xavier grumbled, rubbing his eyes, followed by an exasperated yawn.

Jared, though excited to see him, shot Charlie an annoyed look. "What took you so long?" he nagged. "It doesn't take eight hours and a graveyard shift to find a precinct!"

As much as Ryland didn't care much for Jared's tone, she couldn't help but echo the same thought. "Yeah, where were you?"

As the eight friends settled into more comfortable positions, Charlie lowered himself by Ryland's feet. He planted his hand on her leg and gazed up at her. "I'm sorry," he said. "I did go to the precinct. But on my way back... I took a detour."

Tathia, glaring at him with a sleepy pout, said, "Clearly, you did. How was it at the North Pole? I better get my full wishlist this year."

Ryland shot her a look, signaling her friend to go easy on him, though she appreciated the support. Turning back to her fiancé, she nudged him to explain himself. "So... what happened?"

Charlie hesitated, a split-second pause that didn't go unnoticed. He glanced over his shoulder, and Ryland could clearly see something spinning in his head. She realized his eyes had landed on Sabrina, who was also engrossed in the moment, waiting intently like the others. Then he looked back at Ryland, now determined to stick with his first mind. "The police told me that there have been similar reports to ours," he revealed. "So, I pressed them for what they knew so far. I made it excruciatingly clear how freaked out you and I were, and that I didn't want to wake up to something unimaginable. It turns out that the reports are coming from the surrounding area."

Ryland could tell he was working hard at his wording. She looked up at Sabrina, whose color had gone pallid, her eyes widened in terror. "So, there *is* someone lurking around the ranch!" she cried.

Desmond wrapped his arms around her, but she had already started to panic. Ryland's heart wrenched at the sight of Sabrina. She opened her mouth to comfort the young Turner, but Charlie's hand gently squeezed her leg, pulling her attention back to him. He shook his head, indicating that there was something else going on, but he didn't dare say more.

Xavier, on the other hand, wasn't satisfied with the information Charlie had given up. "So, what did you do?" he demanded. "Are the authorities doing anything about it?"

"Yeah," Charlie answered, his tone even and unaffected. "There's an open case they're looking into, and those strings have everything to do with it."

"And?" Jared pressed.

All Charlie could do was shrug. "That's all the information they gave me." But Ryland knew Charlie too well; she sensed he was holding something back.

Somehow, their friends bought the story he was selling. Desmond, however, asked, "So, why were you gone all these hours?"

Charlie turned away from the faces staring at him intently. His hand slid up to his head, gripping the roots of his hair. "I needed to clear my mind," he said. "This is all just too much."

It was then that Ryland finally caught on. So she said to their friends, "Let's try to get some sleep. I don't think there's anything else we can do at this point."

"Uh uh!" Cheyenne immediately rejected. Pulling up a quilt she'd fished from her overnight bag, she said, "I'm not going back out there. Not until the sun comes up."

Tathia joined in. "I'm with Cheyenne on this one."

Xavier dropped whatever he was feeling at the moment and placed a hand on Charlie's shoulder, who looked at him, surprised. "Let's keep watch for the rest of the night," he suggested. "That way, if anyone tries anything, there's more of us versus them."

The rest of the guys in the room agreed, and so did Charlie. The dark-haired beau rose to his feet and headed toward the direction of his and Ryland's bedroom. He wished everyone a goodnight, but his eyes lingered on the scarlet rose, as if beckoning her to follow him. On cue, she bid goodnight to their friends as well and headed for their room. Tathia briefly stopped her. With a comforting glint dancing in her eyes, she said, "At least he came back, right?"

Ryland flashed an appreciative smile and gave a curt, agreeable nod before ducking into the bedroom. As soon as she stepped inside, Charlie closed the door and placed his hands on her shoulders. Before she realized what was happening, he pulled her farther from the door until they were standing at the very end of their room. Ryland shot him a bewildered look, prompting him to start talking.

Charlie raised his hands, realizing what he'd just done. "I didn't mean to scare you," he said, his voice so low that Ryland sort of wished he'd chosen the volume of a whisper. "I just don't want the others to find out what I'm about to tell you." Then he flicked back his denim jacket, revealing two files he'd tucked into his belt. He grabbed those, then reached for the inner pocket of his jacket, where he fished out a plastic bag packed with red strings. Ryland felt as if she were about to fall through the floor. She started to inch away, weary of how to digest what she was seeing. But when she looked into Charlie's eyes, she saw the cloud of fear hovering over his umber pools. Still, she was too rattled to speak. He summoned the strength to explain what was happening around them.

Lifting the bag of strings in the air, he said, "I found these in Maxwell's desk."

"What!" erupted from her lips, causing Charlie to flinch. "Are you crazy? What if you got caught!"

"Shh! Keep it down!" he scolded, looking back at the door. He took a moment to check around it. Then he locked it before returning to her. "*I had to*," he protested. "There's more to those police reports—starting with what they have in common."

Ryland arched her brows, urging him to spill.

"Almost every one of the reports has an association with the ranch."

Those words hit Ryland so hard, the room started to spin. Her hands clenched onto his dark gray jacket, though a part of her found that ironic, considering that Charlie was standing right in front of her. She swallowed back a new level of fear trying to barge through the walls of her mind. "What kind of association?" she asked.

Charlie sucked in a breath. "Most of them are clients." Then he whipped out the two stacked manila folders. "These are our files. Something led me to look into them, and I found all of our information. I mean *all* of it. From where we went to school—and I mean going back to kindergarten—to our credit scores, our addresses... Just stuff I highly doubt has anything to do with treatment. I don't want to jump to conclusions, but"—he waved the folders and bag of strings in the air—"this is beyond scary!"

Ryland hung her head, shame and guilt flooding her all over again. Before she knew it, the same tears from all those days ago poured down her face. "I can't believe I got us into this," she cried. "I'm so, so sorry. I messed up."

Charlie leaned closer and kissed her cheek, letting his lips linger there, pouring his love on her mending wounds. When he finally pulled away, he said, "Ryland, I assure you that none of this has anything to do with you, except for us being here. These people need to be brought to their knees. I'm heading back to the police station with all this evidence."

Ryland knew exactly who he was referring to. She didn't protest his plan to return to the precinct, though she had one concern. "What if you get in trouble for taking those?" she asked, nodding at the evidence in his hands.

"Then I do," he said. "At least the police will have all the leads they need."

It *was* a risky plan, but Ryland decided to make peace with it.

CHAPTER TWENTY-THREE

The sun finally broke through the horizon, its rays streaming through all the windows of the cabin, rousing all eight friends from their sleep. Ryland and Charlie guided their friends to the door, but not before thanking them for their support. As soon as they were all gone, the couple prepared for the day together. Once Charlie was ready, he set out with the overall plan to head back to the precinct. He comforted the scarlet rose with an embrace, letting his warmth wash over her. She wanted to stay that way, but she knew he had to go. So as he walked out the door, she watched him disappear down the dirt path, back in the direction where she knew he had parked the Silverado.

Once he was out of view, the fiery belle was sparked with an agenda of her own. In the full-body mirror engraved in the closet door of their bedroom, she took one last sweep of the dark blue flannel she wore for her plan. But she couldn't resist slipping into her favorite ripped black skinny jeans. Instead of throwing her hair into another sloppy bun, she let her straightened crimson tresses flow to the small of her back. Then she put on a light layer of makeup to give herself a polished look. She walked out the door in mid-rise black booties, her shoulders rolled back. As she trekked down the path to the morning session, butterflies resurfaced and fluttered about her insides. But they gradually succumbed to the new kind of fire kindling within.

Ryland allowed herself to go through the motions, despite the questionable glances floating her way from Sherrie. Even Cheyenne and Xavier marveled at the sudden shift within her. "I always love it when you dress up!" Cheyenne complimented, unable to keep herself from breaking the silent rule as soon as the circle filled the room.

For a moment, that warmed Ryland. How could she let this ranch take away another thing she loved most—fashion? Nonetheless, the bit of triumph simmered when Sherrie dismissed the group for the day. Taking this as her chance, the scarlet rose walked right up to Sherrie, who was visibly surprised at her willful approach.

"Oh, hi!" the Turner greeted, her voice a bit too pitched. "Don't you look different today?"

Ryland flashed a small smile, though it was far from demure, and let her eyes soften. "Do you have a moment to talk today?"

A glint danced in Sherrie's eyes. "Yes, of course! I have time now! Want to meet back at my office?"

Ryland nodded insistently.

So Sherrie led the scarlet rose back to her home, and into the same office she'd been in before. Ryland took her place on the onyx couch again, while Sherrie sat behind her desk. Once settled with her notebook out and pen in hand, she asked, "What do you want to talk about?"

Ryland sucked in a breath, sifting through her mind for wisdom before speaking another word. In the meantime, she replied, "I've been thinking a lot about the things you've said to me. I have to admit that they're starting to impact me."

That erupted a cheer from Sherrie. "I'm so happy to hear it!" She bounced out of her seat and sat beside the crimson beauty, still holding her notebook. "So, tell me… where are you now? In terms of you and Charlie…?"

That gave Ryland enough material to work with. "That's the thing," she began. "I don't think he's on the same page anymore. He's completely pulled away from the program."

Sherrie's face twisted into a pout, though Ryland's stomach churned at how cartoonish she looked. "That's the hard part about this job," Sherrie continued. "It's hard to see a couple not make it to the end. We try to offer so much here."

Ryland nodded, feigning a bittersweet smile. "Yeah, I guess some processes actually pull people apart rather than bring them together," she said, cringing at how she sounded like Sherrie's echo chamber.

"So, what's the game plan?" Sherrie asked. "We also help divorcees. I mean, I know you two aren't yet married, but I can make things work for you here."

"I'd appreciate that…" Ryland replied, tilting her head as if she were genuinely touched by Sherrie's attempt at empathy. "I'm thinking I need time to heal. Closure, even…"

"Yes, closure is always the key to building back up from a broken relationship," said Sherrie. "Maybe someday, you'll find another guy who is willing to see you for you, and not his vision."

Ryland fought an eye roll. She so badly wanted to rain on Sherrie's parade by listing all the ways Charlie had always given her room to blossom. She wanted to spill how Charlie could bring healing in a matter of moments, compared to the two-week attempt that had only turned Ryland's mind into a hell of its own. Instead, she said, "I trust that I'll have the right guy by my side in the end."

Even then, Ryland didn't miss the twitch in Sherrie's brow as her grin began to strain. Still, Sherrie maintained her composure, saying, "For now, let's redirect the focus to enjoying your own company. It's time to build yourself into the person you were meant to be."

The scarlet rose stared blankly, realizing how often Sherrie had said that to her. So, she asked, "Who am I supposed to be? You seem to be the only one to see potential in me. What do I have potential for?"

Sherrie raised a hand to her chest and rested the other on Ryland's shoulder. "That's a step in the right direction," she said, instead of giving a direct answer. "We have to always be willing to ask ourselves these questions. The more you do that, the more doors you open and find yourself on the path to a better and successful you."

Of course, Ryland thought. Another sugarcoated promise. But Sherrie did give the scarlet rose exactly what she was looking for. Her heart started to see the truth, but she needed something tangible to prove she wasn't imagining it—even if the outright proof revealed itself in another conversation of sweet nothings. So, Ryland flashed another honeyed grin and said, "Thank you for helping me sort things out."

Sherrie mirrored the smile as they both rose to their feet. "I'm glad this was helpful," she told Ryland. "You can come to me and Maxwell anytime. Our doors are always open for you." Then, with a playful grin, she added, "For now, I'd love to stay and chat... but Max and I have a beautiful lunch date by the east side lake. I've been looking forward to it all week!"

The words pierced Ryland. Though she laughed along with Sherrie, her heart tightened. With Sherrie's emerald eyes sparkling and her demeanor so buoyant, Ryland couldn't help but wonder how someone could be so oblivious—how they could work to unravel other couples and then proudly boast about their own happiness, ignoring the broken heart standing right in front of them.

It was downright cruel.

Ryland tried to shake it off and walk away, but it turned out that she and Sherrie were heading in the same direction. Part of her opted for silence, but she quickly realized that would invite pure torment. So instead, as they strolled down the dirt path back toward the heart of the ranch, Ryland asked, "How long have you been married?"

With the same grin still dancing on her face, Sherrie replied, "It's been about thirty years. It feels like forever, honestly."

"Wow…" escaped Ryland, and she meant it. It was encouraging to meet a couple who had been married for so long. She prayed often for her and Charlie's relationship to endure just as long. Preferably, even longer.

"Want to know when I realized he was the one?"

That captured Ryland's attention, and she nodded eagerly. She couldn't help it—she was captivated by love. Yet, listening to someone like Sherrie speak of such a thing felt like a betrayal to her own heart. A part of her wanted to turn away, but despite the unease, she found herself leaning in, willing to listen.

Sherrie continued, "I met him back in high school. I was a junior, and he was a senior. He was the quarterback of the football team, one of the stars of our school. You know, the classic American boy—blue-eyed, blonde, with a smile that could knock a girl off her feet. I have to admit, I was one of them. Every time I saw him in the halls or in the cafeteria, chatting with the popular kids—especially those really pretty girls—just looking at him left me breathless."

Ryland could easily picture it. Her mind tugged her back to those early days with Charlie, when they were new to each other. With each moment they shared, they were slowly interwoven, two souls gradually becoming one.

"My mother once told me that you'd know when you met the person you were meant to be with," Sherrie went on. "One day, I was sitting in the bleachers with a couple of friends, watching the boys practice. Then he walked up to me. I was shocked when he asked me to go to prom with him—the quiet girl who always had her head buried in books. I'd never felt more special..."

As Sherrie continued, Ryland found it harder to stomach each word. Here was a woman who extolled the beauty of love, yet actively denied it to couples like her own daughter and Desmond, like Lydia and Adam. A new kind of anger surged through Ryland, burning through her veins. Her brown eyes hardened, and her jaw clenched in resolve as she prepared to say everything on her mind.

But before the fiery belle could utter a single word, Sherrie let out a blood-curdling shriek that sent a chill slicing down Ryland's spine. Sherrie's hands flew to her mouth as she froze, her wide-eyed gaze fixed toward the buildings where group sessions and workshops were held. Ryland followed her stare and felt a jolt of shock ripple through her as she saw a swarm of people in midnight blue and solid black uniforms. A few wore lighter uniforms, their vests laden with all kinds of tactical gear. Charlie's face immediately surfaced in her mind.

Both women rushed toward the unfolding chaos. The cluster of authorities soon mingled with bewildered faces in flannel, their expressions a patchwork of confusion and fear. Ryland stopped short, holding herself back from venturing further, her breaths shallow and strained. Sherrie, lost in disarray, plunged into the crowd, her frantic pleas echoing in the air before dissolving into incoherent bluster. A few of the officers pivoted in Ryland's direction. She braced herself for interrogation, her heart pounding. But they brushed past her, their purposeful strides aimed at the Turner home atop the hill.

Then, familiar faces came into view. Though their features were painted with panic, a spark of relief lit their eyes as they spotted her.

"You're okay!" exclaimed Cheyenne, yanking Ryland into her arms. "We thought something happened to you!"

"I'm okay," Ryland assured her, though the pandemonium around her left her dazed and disoriented.

Jared scanned the crowd, his voice tight with urgency. "Where is Charlie?"

Desmond's eyes widened. "Did something happen to him?"

Ryland somewhat shook her head, half of her mind being gnawed at. She scanned the crowd, hoping his face would appear, but he was nowhere to be found. Her shoulders slumped as a sinking realization washed over her.

Sabrina, sensing the heaviness shadowing Ryland, reached out. "Hey, talk to us..." she coaxed. "What's going on?"

Instead of responding to Sabrina, Ryland sought out one of the officers, hoping at least one of them would recognize her fiancé's name. Just as she stepped toward one, a familiar set of arms wrapped around her from behind, pulling her close. As soon as she felt his embrace, tears spilled down her cheeks, relief flooding her like a wave. She spun around, and there he was—the only face she wanted to see.

Charlie flashed a triumphant smile, his deep sienna eyes and ebony hair catching the sunlight. Her gaze fell to the gold cross resting on his chest, revealed through his half-buttoned white linen shirt. His hands rose to her face, the cool metal of his rings soothing her flushed cheeks in the midday heat. His presence was an anchor, grounding her amidst the chaos.

Sabrina stepped forward, her countenance tender but weighed down. "What's happening?" she pleaded.

Charlie heaved a sigh, reluctant to say what he knew would hurt her. "Your parents have been on the police's radar for a long time," he confessed.

"What?" gasped the group, their faces blanched with disbelief. Sabrina's face went pallid, her body trembling as she absorbed the news. "That can't be..." she whispered, grasping for denial.

But the truth was unyielding. "I'm sorry," said Charlie. "For fourteen years, your parents have been evading the law. They're wanted for fraudulent documents, false imprisonment, and a string of lawsuits from clients whose marriages were destroyed..."

A stunned silence hung over them, the weight of revelation pressing down. The friends stood paralyzed, each lost in a storm of unspoken thoughts.

Then, Sabrina broke. She collapsed into Desmond's arms, her tears an anguished torrent. The group watched her fall apart, her sobs muffled against Desmond's shoulder. Tathia placed a hand on her back, offering what comfort she could. Cheyenne and Xavier looked particularly stricken, grappling with the unsettling reality that two people they had trusted to heal relationships had instead shattered them. Yet, amidst the heartbreak, Ryland felt a flicker of joy watching the husband and his lavender-haired wife console each other, their silent reassurance a testament to the genuine love they shared.

Sabrina finally lifted her head, her tear-streaked face etched with betrayal. "That's why they dragged me all the way out here..." she whispered, her voice trembling with fury. "They tore me from my childhood and my friends back in Palm Springs for this." She looked at Charlie, desperation in her eyes. "That's what you're telling me?"

All Charlie could do was nod, offering her an apologetic shrug. "I wish it weren't true," he said softly. "But the last center they ran... I can't even repeat those stories. They marked their victims with red strings, posed as perfect partners, then tore into their clients' lives.

Some people lost their minds, others suffered tragic divorces. The ones who survived were the ones who managed to sue."

Desmond's hazel eyes hardened, directing a glare at Sherrie, now being escorted in handcuffs. "All Sabrina and I wanted was to get married," he muttered, almost to himself. "I left my home, jumped through hoops—just for their approval." His voice cracked. "I can't believe I let myself get... manipulated like that."

Ryland shook her head, refusing to let him shoulder that guilt. "They targeted all of us: the young, the vulnerable, the broken."

"Or all three," Sabrina murmured, her cheek pressed against Desmond's shoulder.

Jared stepped forward, his arm protectively around Tathia. "We need to get out of here. I don't want to stay in this place a second longer." The rest of the group voiced their agreement.

Ryland looked up at Charlie, her eyes pleading. "Take me home."

Without hesitation, Charlie gathered his fiancée and their friends, guiding them away from the chaos, away from the storm that had cast its shadow over them for far too long. As the couple and their friends folded into their cars, Ryland leaned back, feeling the weight lift from her shoulders. For the first time in a long while, her mind was clear. The fires that had once threatened to consume her had finally been extinguished. Now, with Charlie by her side, they could begin to rebuild, stone by stone, a foundation stronger than anything that had come before.

At last, she could look forward to a true oasis with him.

EPILOGUE

Hand in hand, dressed in a satin white gown, the scarlet rose had fully bloomed in the weeks leading to this moment. The serendipitous air of romance painted her cheeks with a soft blush, her heart resting securely in Charlie's hands, just as his was in hers. It was a beautiful exchange before the altar—a promise woven into their vows, both of them eager for the veil to fall and bring them even closer. As they slid their eternity rings onto each other's fingers, they sealed their covenant with a kiss.

A chorus of cheers erupted from their friends and family, filling the room with warmth and joy.

As they pulled apart, Ryland's eyes sparkled like stars, brightened by the glint of tiny rhinestones carefully dusted across her eyeliner. Charlie, too, seemed lost in her, his deep russet orbs lingering as though he were seeing her for the first time. The conviction in his eyes stirred her deeply; every trial, every hardship, felt worth it.

The reception was just as enthralling.

The couple mingled with their guests, savoring every second. While chatting with Callie and David and holding a playful Nathaniel in her arms, Ryland spotted Mama approaching. A knowing smile tugged at her lips as she took in her mother's familiar turtleneck style, though she had to give her credit for dressing in white. Like a little girl, she let herself lean into the warmth of her mother's embrace.

"I'm so proud of you!" Mama exclaimed, her words lingering in the air.

Stunned, Ryland pulled back. "You are?" she asked, her tone tinged with disbelief.

Mama's face softened, understanding written all over it. "I am," she affirmed. "I'm sorry I let my jealousy get in the way."

"Jealous?" Ryland echoed, a slight furrow forming on her brow.

Mama nodded. "When you told me you were engaged, I felt it," she confessed. "Everything I said that night came from the bitterness of watching my own marriage crumble. It felt so unfair, seeing you get something I once longed for but lost." Then she paused, catching herself before delving too deep. "I should have celebrated you."

A new feeling washed over Ryland as her mother's words sank in. It was something close to reprieve. "You're celebrating me now," she said. "That's all I could ever ask for."

Mama's eyes brightened. She stirred to say more when a familiar chorus of voices interrupted. Tathia, Cheyenne, and Sabrina rushed over, practically bouncing with excitement, fawning over Ryland's dress and marveling at how radiant she and Charlie looked together.

"So, can we talk about baby names now?" Tathia teased, though her tone held a touch of sincerity.

"Ooh, I have a few!" Callie inserted.

Ryland laughed, sharing in their joy. "Why not?" she replied, letting her friends and family toss around ideas. The exchange soon turned into a playful debate, as they wondered whether the newlyweds would have a boy or a girl. Deep down, Ryland didn't care. Her heart had already chosen the name she wanted for her child, Azariah—a name that reminded her of Yahweh's presence through every trial, heartbreak, and milestone in her life.

Then Sabrina gently pulled Ryland aside to a quieter corner of the hall. "May I ask you something?" she began, her tone tinged with anticipation.

"Of course," Ryland welcomed her. "What is it?"

Sabrina's face lit up as she lifted her left hand, revealing a radiant-cut diamond resting on her ring finger. A gasp escaped Ryland. As pure joy flooded her, she threw her arms around Sabrina, feeling like a proud older sister. Then, in a voice as delicate as it was fervent, Sabrina popped the question that swelled Ryland's heart.

"Will you be my maid of honor?"

The redhead bobbed her head. "Of course!" she exclaimed without hesitation, her smile as wide as the imaginings of Sabrina on her big day. "I'd love that!"

As they pulled back from one another, a giddy grin spread across Sabrina's face. "Good," she said, "because Desmond already asked Charlie to be his best man."

Ryland's gaze instinctively searched for Charlie, finding him laughing as he watched Xavier and Desmond dance away. Jared lingered nearby, visibly embarrassed by their antics. Then, as if on cue, the music shifted from an upbeat retro rhythm to the soft sway of a ballad that only the newlyweds recognized. Charlie's eyes found her across the room, and their gazes locked, a silent invitation passing between them. With a subtle nod, he beckoned her near.

Sabrina's voice brought Ryland back to the moment. "I love the way you two look at each other." Her green eyes sparkled like a deep shade of period as she added, "Don't ever lose that."

Ryland turned back to her friend, a confident smile gracing her lips. "Trust me, that will never happen."

288